LAST HOUSE BEFORE THE MOUNTAIN

LAST HOUSE BEFORE THE MOUNTAIN

a novel

MONIKA HELFER

TRANSLATED BY GILLIAN DAVIDSON

BLOOMSBURY PUBLISHING

NEW YORK · LONDON · OXFORD · NEW DELHI · SYDNEY

BLOOMSBURY PUBLISHING
Bloomsbury Publishing Inc.
1385 Broadway, New York, NY 10018, USA

BLOOMSBURY, BLOOMSBURY PUBLISHING, and the Diana logo
are trademarks of Bloomsbury Publishing Plc

First published in 2020 in Germany as *Die Bagage*
by Carl Hanser Verlag GmbH & Co. KG
German language edition © 2020 by Carl Hanser Verlag GmbH & Co. KG, Munich
First published in Great Britain 2023
First published in the United States 2023

ISBN: HB: 978-1-63557-987-1; EBOOK: 978-1-63557-988-8

Library of Congress Cataloging-in-Publication Data is available.

2 4 6 8 10 9 7 5 3 1

Typeset by Integra Software Services Pvt. Ltd.
Printed and bound in the U.S.A.

To find out more about our authors and books visit www.bloomsbury.com
and sign up for our newsletters.

Bloomsbury books may be purchased for business or promotional use. For
information on bulk purchases please contact Macmillan Corporate and
Premium Sales Department at specialmarkets@macmillan.com.

Die Bagage (-n)
1. Baggage
2. (pej.) Rabble, shower, *die ganze Bagage* (informal) – the whole lot of them

für meine Bagage
for my Bagage

Here, get the colouring pens out. Draw a small house, with a stream a little bit below it, a water trough. But don't draw the sun; the house actually lies in shadow! Behind it, the mountain − like an upright rock. In front of the house, a woman standing tall, hanging the washing out on the line. The line loops between two cherry trees, one to the right of the veranda leading to the front door, the other to the left. Right now, the woman is carefully pinning up a romper suit and a small jacket, so she must have children. She does the washing frequently, her children's clothes and those of her husband and her own things. She has a particularly beautiful white blouse. She would like her family to be clean like the families in the town. She owns many white things; they set off her dark hair and dark eyes and the dark hair and dark eyes of her husband. The others down in the village rarely wear white, many not even on Sundays. She has a serious face, deep eyes. Draw the eyes with the charcoal pencil. Her hair lies flat on her head. It is black, mixed with brown, because the point of the charcoal pencil has broken off. Good colouring pens aren't shiny, and they are expensive as well.

Reality breezes its way into the picture, cold and pitiless; even soap needs to be rationed. The family is poor, just two cows, one goat. Five children. The man, black-haired like his wife, brilliantly glossy hair too. Quite a looker he is, twice as good-looking as the others. He has a narrow face, but no sign of joyfulness about him. The woman is only just thirty. She knows that she appeals to men; she can't think of a single one that she is unsure of. When her husband pulls her to him, senses her breasts and her belly – this is exactly how he said it – he virtually blacks out, and he flops onto the bed in exhaustion. She undresses hastily, lies down beside him and knows he is only making out that he is asleep. He doesn't want to fail. That's why she has kept her thin undergarment on. So that things are not completely predictable. She looks out through the open window at the night sky. Even the moon remains hidden behind the mountain. Sometimes, it moves quickly past, then she can see the glow above the crest. From time to time a child shouts, she knows which one, then another starts to cry, she knows which one. But she can't manage to get herself out of bed, not that she is tired. She thinks, it's just that I'm lazy. How old am I going to get, she thinks.

The girl, two years old, stands by the bed in the middle of the night. It is Margarethe. Grete. She is shivering.

'Mama,' she whispers.

Mama whispers back, 'Come over here!'

The child goes to her and creeps under the blanket. Father is not to know about this. The child doesn't settle down between her parents, she lies at the edge of the bed. She has to be held firm so that she doesn't fall out, down onto the floor, as the bed is really quite high.

The child was my mother, Margarethe, a timid girl, who, every time she encountered her father, cowered away looking for her mother's skirt. Her father was loving towards the other four children. Overall, he was a loving person, and towards the two children who came along later, he was the same. Just this girl, Margarethe, who was to become my mother, he could not abide, because he believed she was not his child. He showed no anger towards her, no rage; he detested her, she disgusted him, had the aura of the interloper about her, her whole life long. He never hit her. Sometimes the other kids. Never Grete. He could not bear to touch her, even in violence. He acted as if she just didn't exist. Up until his death, he exchanged not a single word with her. And as far as she knew, he had never looked at her. That's what my mother told me, when I was just eight years old. My grandfather wanted to have nothing to do with the shy one. This was the reason why my grandmother cuddled the shy one more than the other children and also loved her more. Maria was the name of my beautiful grandmother, the one whom all the men would have run after, if they hadn't been afraid of her husband.

But I am getting ahead of myself. This story actually begins when my mother had not yet been born. The story begins when she had not even been conceived. It begins on an afternoon when Maria was once again pegging the washing on the line. It was early September, 1914. She saw the postman down on the path. She saw him first from a long way off.

From the farm you had a view down into the valley as far as the church tower that rose up above the lime trees. The postman was pushing his bike because the path up to the small house climbed steeply and after the turnoff it was only roughly gravelled. The man was exhausted. He wanted to be called *Adjunkt*; *Postadjunkt* was the official title for his job as assistant postmaster. He wore a uniform with shiny buttons. He was sweating, had loosened his tie, opened his collar. He doffed his cap briefly in greeting and for a bit of air. Maria took a step backwards as he handed the letter to her. It was a blue letter with a tear-off slip on the front. The slip had to be signed and returned to the sender. The sender was the State, it wanted proof of delivery. The Adjunkt knew that she knew that he liked her and even more than that. He also knew that she was indifferent towards him. He wasn't half as handsome as Josef, her husband, with his dark looks, if handsomeness can actually be halved or doubled.

The Adjunkt disapproved of the way the men in the village talked about Josef and Maria. Children didn't prove anything, at any rate, whether one was good at it or just able to have them, even having four children meant absolutely nothing. A woman can give birth, even if her husband doesn't satisfy her. That is nature's way and nature has nothing to do with love, and just because one happens to be called Josef and Maria, that says nothing at all, rather the opposite. The men would have liked it to be that way. For as they saw it, they themselves might then get the chance to have a go with the lovely Maria. The couple were hardly ever seen coming into the village together, and from this the men drew their conclusions yet again and took it as further evidence. And when they were seen, they were not companionable with each other, did not look at each other, Josef nearly always serious and usually Maria as well, as if they had just had a quarrel. But the men were mistaken. If truth be told,

Maria enjoyed lying held tightly in Josef's embrace. She was passionate. And sometimes her husband was too. When they lay with each other, it was not as if they blew out the light. Definitely not. And after they had blown out the light, they might talk together for a long while.

The Adjunkt delivered only once a week so far out, because it was so far uphill and arduous. And Maria was seldom on her own and seldom out in the front of the house. Often before, he had knocked at the door and no one had opened up. And why trudge up that path over and over for nothing? He would have preferred it if the people who lived up here, scattered about, had friends down in the village, at least one person they could trust, that he could deliver their letters to, and then they could pick them up themselves. A letter from the State of course had to be received in person. At least I'll get to see her today, thought the Adjunkt to himself.

The area belonging to the village was extensive, the most outlying farm a good hour's distance from the church. Six farms lay on the outskirts, behind them rose the lower slopes of the mountain. Things were not good between those who lived at its foot, in its shadow, and those down in the village. And even among themselves things were not good. Things not being good meant not wanting to know how the other person was doing – nothing else. They lived there because their forefathers arrived later than the others and the land was the cheapest, and the land was the cheapest because it needed such hard labour. Maria and Josef lived right at the end up there with their family. People called them '*die Bagage*'.

Originally the word meant simply 'the bearers', referring to the fact that Josef's father and grand-father had been itinerant labourers, men who were not bound to anyone, had no fixed roof over their heads, who moved from one farm to another asking for work, and in summer carried hayricks taller than a man into the farmers' barns. That was the most menial of all occupations, lower than a farm hand. It was later that the name '*Bagage*' took on a differ-ent meaning, morphed into its pejorative sense – 'the undesirables' or 'riff-raff'.

The letter came from the army. Bearing call-up papers. Austria had declared war against Serbia, and Russia had risen to the defence of Serbia, and the German emperor had risen to the defence of Austria, and France had risen to the defence of Russia and declared war against Germany and Austria, and Germany had marched into Belgium.

The Adjunkt was still holding the blue letter in his hand. He daydreamed to himself that he was looking after her; something might happen and he would look after her and she would finally recog-nise what sort of person he really was. He would have liked to liberate her from her husband, for he imagined that she had a hard time with him, and he imagined that he himself was the sort of man who could show a lot of tender affection if it came to it, and not just for a short time, not just for one night or so but 'until death us do part'. She didn't have any red patches on her face or on her neck. He couldn't see the tiniest wrinkle, not between her eyebrows, nor at the sides of her mouth, and no sign of crow's feet around her eyes. Her hands were rough, but only on the inside. On the back they were a smooth gold. Her husband was often out of town. He had various business affairs. What sort of affairs, the Adjunkt did not know, and Maria didn't know about them either. It was assumed in the village that they were some sort of underhand, crooked deals. Josef had the reputation of resorting immediately to his fists. But the men used this as an excuse, a means of justifying their cowardice to themselves. That up till now, none of them had dared to approach Maria directly. For the very reason that Josef was the sort of man who lashed out aggressively straightaway. Mind you, no one had actually witnessed him lashing out.

The letter was from the army, said the Adjunkt, Maria had to confirm receipt with her signature. In brackets, she should write 'Spouse'. He had an indelible pencil with him, she was welcome to use it. He licked the end of the pencil for her.

Maria knew that there was a war on, but up till now it had never crossed her mind that it would ever have any effect on her, that they would hear of it up and down the remotest valley in the shadow of the mountain. She could not say in detail what was in the printed letter, but one thing was clear: Josef Moosbrugger had to go to war.

The mayor's name was Gottlieb Fink, and he also had various business affairs. He was the only one with whom Josef exchanged more than the most necessary conversation. Anything more than just: yes, no, morning, and again, yes and no. Sometimes Josef had come down from the mountain and gone direct to the mayor's house and had walked in without knocking or calling to him, and had stayed in the house for a good hour. But the two were not friends. The mayor would have liked to have been a friend of Josef Moosbrugger. He was the only person that one could talk to. Firstly, he was not sick, secondly, he didn't stink like an animal, and thirdly, he was not an idiot. He could read and write and could calculate figures better than most. Give him the most difficult multiplication, he would roll his eyes once and give you the answer. The mayor was generous. He always shared the proceeds of his business deals, even on the occasions when Josef had not had much input. Always fifty-fifty. Josef was not so generous. But the mayor never held this against him. The mayor had cows, pigs, hens and a couple of goats, like everyone else out here, but in addition he had a workshop attached to his house. He was a qualified gunsmith. In the past, he used to turn and file down the gun barrels himself and saw the wood for the butt, carve it, oil and polish it, all himself. Nowadays he sourced the parts from south Germany and just assembled them. That was cheaper and more profitable. He affixed his stamp to them. The gun was then a genuine Fink, and Fink hunting guns still had a good reputation, just as if they were individually fashioned and finished by hand. The mayor had given Josef a hunting gun as a gift, in fact, a double-barrelled one. That was more than generous. Everyone was surprised by this. That said everything, although no one could say, exactly, what it said. A furniture maker would have had to work more than six months to have one of those. Maybe Josef really was his friend. Just because he always made out that he didn't need friends, that was far from meaning that he truly had no need of one.

When the call-up papers arrived, Josef needed a friend. The mayor had not been called up, the reason being that he was needed at home. That was true: for example, Josef needed him.

Josef loved his wife. He himself had never uttered this word. This word did not exist in every-day speech. It was not possible to say, '*I love you*', in everyday speech. For that reason, he had never even contemplated this word. Maria belonged to him. And he wanted her to be his and to belong to him, the former meaning in bed and the latter as family. When he walked through the village and saw the men by the well, playing with wooden knives that they had carved themselves, and when he saw that they saw him, he could read in their eyes: You are Maria's husband. All of them had wondered what it would be like to be with her. And now that he had received his call-up, they were thinking opportunities might be opening up. Modest opportunities because no one knew exactly how long the war would last; even if the word from Vienna and Berlin was that it would soon be over, no one was taking any bets.

Josef went to the mayor and said: 'Could you watch out for Maria while I am away at the front?'

The mayor knew how 'watch out for' in this case was to be interpreted. In the first place, he was thinking, Josef means that he can't trust his wife. Can she trust herself? That was the question! She sees herself every morning in the mirror.

No one else was present during this conversation. A delicate conversation to be had in private. How could the mayor answer my grandmother's husband? Would he have the confidence to say: 'You mean, you want me to see that no one goes up to her place when you are away?'

And Josef? If he said: 'Yes, that's what I mean,' then he would be admitting that he didn't trust his wife.

Josef said: 'Yes, I'd be grateful if you could see no one goes up there to her.'

'And why?' the mayor might ask. But doing that would offend Josef. He doesn't want to do that. Is it likely that one of the men from the village or from some other place might assault the lovely Maria? That in such a case the mayor would have to step in? And what would that mean? That he had to shoot the man dead?

The mayor said: 'I'll look after her. You don't need to worry while you are away at war, Josef.'

Can it be, that such a beautiful woman is meant for just one man? The mayor thought that Maria was faithful only out of fear of her husband and not because of indifference to other men. There was no need to make a big to-do about it, if one or other of the men was reckoning that Josef might fall, that's human nature. Of course, the mayor would not have said this to Josef. Particularly because he wanted to keep him as a friend. He was the mayor and it was his wish that not a single person from his village would be missing when this war was over. Anyway, in his opinion, it did no harm having a good-looking friend and the Lady Mayor was of the same opinion; she thought that Josef made him look good. Actually, she liked Josef rather a lot. As she said herself quite openly, she would love to see Josef naked just once, preferably alone out in the woods. Clearly there was no danger of this happening, otherwise she would have kept her mouth shut. No one needs to keep an eye on my wife, thought the mayor, and even if I were called up, no one would need to keep an eye on her. The mayor enjoyed being married. He and his wife were known for being great fun, not only in the small village but right through the whole valley as far as Bregenz. And this was mainly due to her. She had an infectious laugh. Even Josef laughed with her, especially when she got into full swing and he had no idea what was coming next.

'I'm afraid it's not possible for her to move down here with us with all the children,' said the mayor, 'though it would probably be better.'

'There's no need,' said Josef. 'It's enough just to keep an eye out. Apparently it will all be over sometime in October. I'll be back then anyway.'

'And you'll get leave too,' said the mayor.

'If everything goes as quickly as they say, they won't be giving any leave.' That was the general belief. In actual fact, Josef would have two spells of leave.

After Josef had said goodbye to his wife with a hug and a light kiss to go off to war – he was already on his way, flexing his knees jauntily on the descent, as was his way – she ran after him and pulled him back into the house and into the bedroom, undid his belt and wrapped herself around him.

'Why are you making such a face?' she asked.

'I've got toothache,' he said.

'But that's going to get worse,' she said.

'There are dentists in the field,' said Josef. 'Apparently far better than in Bregenz.'

'How did you find that out?'

He stood up from the bed and held her back from his body. She should stop asking questions, he knew how that went. She would carry on and he would get there too late.

Not many men from the village were called up at the beginning of September. Why my grandfather was in the first group, I have no idea. There were just four of them, one was called Franz, like the emperor, one Ludwig, one Alois and then Josef. They were supposed to go on foot to the village after next. There, they would be picked up by truck and brought to the station in Bregenz, and then off into the field, where and however that might be. In the end, only one of the four did not die on the battlefield: Josef. Alois was dead just one week later. Ludwig died in a field hospital after six months. Franz fell a year later at Valparola Pass. Five more lads followed afterwards, and of those only two returned.

The four men had stuck flowers in their hats and stood there getting steaming drunk. The mayor, as representative of the emperor, gave away schnapps and let off a shot into the air. A crowd of children accompanied the lottery lads, as the conscripts were called. But they only marched as far as the next village, then turned back. The future soldiers went onwards from there on their own, further on to L., not in march step, and they had stopped singing and had more or less sobered up. They talked about things that needed to be done and that they wanted to get done soon, as if they would be back home again in a matter of days or weeks. They plucked the flowers out of their hats and tossed them beside the path. Now that there was no one they knew to see them, why bother?

Josef's second son, the headstrong Lorenz, just nine years old, went along with the others to the next village. He was clever – in school his ability to count in his head left his teacher thrilled and in awe. This was a gift inherited from his father. He was already discontented with life in the mountains. He had no desire to be a farmer. Just the fact that he contemplated what he might become one day set him apart from all the other lads in the village. He was interested in motor cars, and there were not many of those in the valley – usually simply known as *the Forest* – and they were always the same ones. His father had patted him on the shoulder, nothing more. That was his farewell. At home Lorenz had to look after the animals, the two cows, the goat. And there was a dog too. They called him 'Wolf'. Father had trained him well. He did not need to be chained up. Father had laid a trail of stones in a line all around the house. The dog did not go beyond this line, no matter what happened. The Postadjunkt was still afraid of him. When Maria saw the postman approaching, she put the dog inside the house. Lorenz would not have done that. He liked the dog, it belonged to the family, and you didn't send a member of the family inside when someone outside the family turned up. Then there was a cat too, who got the scraps when there were leftovers, and if there were no leftovers, she had to sort herself out.

Lorenz drove the cows out into the meadow, it was already far too late but the day had started in an unusual way. Before Father had set off, Heinrich, the oldest child of Maria and Josef, had milked the cows and the goat. Then Father had washed himself slowly from top to bottom, including his hair. Mama had brought the children inside, she didn't want them to see their father naked. The goat stayed night and day within the fence. Lorenz gave her a load of hay, gazing into the crossbeams of her eyes. And thought to himself what he always thought when he stood in front of the goat: why don't all of us have the same eyes? The cat has vertical slits, the goat crossbeams and humans have circular sockets.

What might he have become, my Uncle Lorenz, if he had not been one of the Bagage children! What might his brothers and sisters have become?

'War is normal,' he once said to me. There was no obvious connection to the conversation he was having at the time, which I had not been party to anyway. When Uncle Lorenz was talking to my father, I was as silent as the umbrella hanging over the back of his chair.

'What do you mean by that?' I asked, after clearing my throat noisily. He had a way of either ignoring me or turning to me suddenly and poking me in the ribs with his index finger. The uncle with charisma. That can be good and yet not good in a person, at the same time.

He answered: 'Well my girl, why would I say something and mean something else? I mean what I say: war is normal.' Had he forgotten my name?

When he visited us, I couldn't be still. I was always on the alert. For something. In the Second World War he had been in Russia. He had a wife at home, and then it turned out he had a wife and child in Russia too, but had left her and made the long journey back to his wife in our country. From time to time a military vehicle had given him a lift; other times he travelled by train without paying, or travelled pillion on a motorbike. Most of the time he walked. He visited us often when I was a child. He played chess with my father. He hated the small-mindedness of country life. He and my father spoke about this. My father also had no time for farmers. He had of course been born to a housemaid in Lungau and his father, one of the well-to-do, had never taken any interest in him. Uncle Lorenz had three children in our country, considered his sons good for nothing, even before they had the chance to be good for something, and in the end they didn't come to anything either; one hanged himself from a tree. Uncle Lorenz freely admitted that a second family existed in Russia. He was fifty years old when a drunk driver ran him over on the bridge over the Rhine in Bregenz, killing him. His dog lay beside him and howled. I named my son after him: 'But I'm not like him and I don't want to be either,' he said.

Heinrich used to help his mother the most. As the story unfolded, he was eleven, two years older than his brother Lorenz. He was the strong, silent type who never wanted to be anything but a farmer. His mama often said to him: 'You're more grown up than I am! Do something crazy at least once in your life, Heinrich!' But he didn't do anything crazy. He wanted to be a farmer so much that he never for a moment contemplated whether something else might perhaps suit him. It got on his nerves the way every minor setback caused Lorenz to question whether things could be different for him. Heinrich counted on his fingers until the end of his life.

Mother, said Father on the evening before he went to war, Mother was only to work in the house. Heinrich and Lorenz were to see to the farming. Katharina, she was ten, helped her mother with the washing and in the kitchen. Walter was still not able to be of any use. He played with the wooden top that Heinrich had carved for him but he never managed to get it to spin properly.

I called Katharina 'Aunt Kathe'. When she died, she was almost one hundred. She dyed her hair black.

She was slim and held herself erect right to the end. She had straight shoulders and if you saw her walking from behind, even when she was eighty, you could have been fooled into thinking, this woman here is forty at most, and judging by the way she walks, she has a zest for life. If you saw her from the front, you might have thought she looked like an American Indian in an old picture. Seeing her from the front, you would be transported into the world of an old black-and-white film, a western, every wrinkle a sharp edge. She had a long, hooked nose and a mouth that always looked as if it wanted to say, *clear off and leave me in peace.* She was fond of my sisters, especially the older one, because she was well-behaved, shy and retiring. She said I was too wild for her, she 'couldn't' with me. I asked her what she meant, what 'couldn't' she with me? She made a slicing motion with her hand through the air, that was it. In late summer she used to send me to collect apples with her son as it grew dark. We were supposed to sneak into the garden of a certain neighbour and shake the Gravenstein tree, fill two rucksacks full of apples and then beat it. I always had a guilty conscience, as if I – yes, I! – had talked Aunt Kathe into this, and her son too, who always looked at me as if I came from a family of villains.

And my Uncle Walter? He drowned in Lake Constance, at the age of forty-two. He was a redhead, he and my mother the only ones in the Bagage clan who were not dark, and he had a pockmarked face and a long head and an upper body that looked as if it had been chiselled by a sculptor in marble. He went after every woman and women seem to have enjoyed his attentions. Besides his fat spouse with the five children, he had a second woman, who was on the game. His wife, for her part, was sleeping with a sales rep for household goods. At some point his lover became too demanding for him and he passed her on to his youngest brother. And then he drowned. Walter had just turned five when his father went off to war.

It was the beginning of September and still very hot, Lorenz took off his shirt and tied it around the waistband of his trousers. His face was serious like his father's, even a bit severe. The dog waited in front of the house. He always placed one paw on the boundary that had been set for him. He had never stepped over the stone markers of his own accord. He squirmed and yowled his high-pitched whines. Lorenz laid a hand on his head.

'Wolf,' he said. 'We're going in a minute.'

Maria was inside; she lay in the bedroom. The double bed took up most of the room. Space had been found for a small wardrobe. The door was open a crack. Lorenz saw his mother lying on her stomach, her head on one arm. He slipped into the hall and climbed up the ladder into the attic. Father had nailed a narrow screen beside one of the rafters. It was hard to tell it was a hiding place. Behind it was the gun. The gift from Gottlieb Fink. And there was ammunition there too. Now, thought Lorenz, now Father gets a weapon from the emperor and this one here, the Fink shotgun, now belongs to me. It belongs to me until Father gets back from the war. He tucked a box with cartridges into his trouser pocket, wrapped the gun in his shirt and climbed down the ladder. He ran out of the house, called the dog, 'Come, Wolf!' The two ran down the slope past the water trough across the path. They crossed the stream, jumping from stone to stone, disappearing up into the woods on the other side of the narrow valley.

Lorenz knew of a good spot. A dip which was not overlooked on either side. Perhaps Mother would hear the shot. Lorenz didn't think it would bother her. Sometimes hunters roamed through the woods. Down in the village no one would hear a thing. He set up a row of fist-sized stones on a bank of moss. At a distance of twenty paces he lay down in the ferns, the weapon in firing position, and fired. Father had shown him how to handle the recoil without it hurting too much. He, Lorenz, was the only one that Father had taken shooting with him. Not Heinrich, the eldest. Lorenz knew why. Heinrich liked animals too much. He could never be made into a hunter. The dog sprang up at the first shot. Lorenz had to calm him down. He put his arm around him, pressed his head down to his. At this distance, he hit the target every time. He emptied the whole box of ammunition. Twenty-five shots. The trigger was on a stiff setting. His finger was sore. That made him happy.

As soon as Josef had taken his leave of Maria, she had fallen on the bed and closed her eyes. Walter lay down across her belly. Although he was already too big and too heavy. He was a friendly child. He even liked lying down beside the dog in his kennel. The dog was fierce like all dogs out here, but Walter could do with him what he wanted, and woe betide anyone who laid a hand on Walter, if they were not family. He even growled if one of the family laid a hand on him.

Katharina was knitting. Her mother had taught her, and she was good at it. The red wool was to be made into a scarf. For Papa. She should hurry up, so she finishes it before the war is over. Mother had seen pictures of soldiers. She liked their blue uniforms; they made even the most unremarkable man look imposing. She had no other thought in mind but that Josef would come home in uniform and red would go very well with blue.

Mother was tired and allowed herself to be tired, now that Father was out of the house, otherwise she would never have lain down on the bed during the day. There was very little to eat. The mayor, who was the most well off, would provide her with food once a week while Father was away. That's what had been agreed. In return, Josef would tweak his accounts for him, when he came back. The children liked the jovial mayor, he whirled Katharina in the air, although she was almost not a child any more, he pretended to be a lion to Walter. He was reticent towards Lorenz, who was too similar to his father. That irritated the mayor.

On the very same day that Josef and the three others set off for the war, the mayor came up to Maria's house. With him he brought potatoes, onions and apples. He had loaded up a barrow and one of the men from the village had wheeled it up, and been sent straight back down again. He himself had come on horseback. They had plenty of their own cherries up there and, what's more, the best ones. Josef had said to Maria she should give the mayor a bag full of cherries because he liked them so much.

The mayor sat down beside Maria in the kitchen. Walter was looking after his horse. Lorenz was helping him – that is how Lorenz expressed it, to please his little brother. The shutters were closed against the hot sun. Crockery was still stacked in the washing bowl. Maria was barefoot. She had tied her hair into a knot.

He would be going at the weekend to L., to the cattle market, said the mayor. He wanted to have a look around for a bull. In wartime, the prices were cheaper. But no one could say for how much longer. In war, normal rules don't apply even in those places where there is no shooting. In the Forest, this he could guarantee, there would be no shooting. But prices even here were wartime prices. He was of the view, said the mayor, that it would make sense to buy a bull for the village now. Each person could pay a set amount and each would have the benefit of it. Where it would be housed in the end, we would have to see. He bet that Josef, if he were here, would say the same. Wouldn't she, Maria, like to come with him to L.? He knew that her sister lived there. She could visit her. And the cattle market was also a bit like the annual fair. Even if one perhaps couldn't buy very much, there was lots to see anyway. It would do her good.

'Then I would have to take the children along,' said Maria, 'that won't work.'

The children could stay with his wife, said the mayor, she loved to have children around more than anything, since she hadn't managed to have a child herself, not a single one.

'To be honest, Maria,' he said, 'I have already spoken to her.' That was the truth, because he had assumed that she would go with him.

Maria wanted to think about it.

She should, if she wanted to, come to their place at half past five in the morning on Thursday with the children. If she wanted to. He would not force anyone.

That was three days away. In truth, Maria was delighted. There would be music, sweet things on sale and people to watch and eavesdrop on. She loved all that. She was also looking forward to seeing her sister. Not as much as the market stalls and the music. Probably a brass band would be playing. On the other hand, she had heard that all the brass bands had been called to the war. But then again, she couldn't imagine that there was much call for music in battle.

Lorenz was furious when his mother explained to him that the Lady Mayor wanted to look after Walter, and the others could go along too.

'That's completely out of the question,' he said. 'We'll look after our brother by ourselves, Heinrich, me and Katharina. Anyway, Walter doesn't need a nursemaid.' He raised his objections to the visit to the cattle market in an indirect way. 'What's the point of a woman going there, you don't have any money.' It was the most ridiculous idea, and what on earth did she want to go there for?

'Hold your tongue, right now,' said Mother. 'You're only nine, you've no right to stop me doing anything!' She saw her husband in Lorenz and it annoyed her.

'Can I at least take Wolf with me to the mayor's?' asked Lorenz. Now he spoke meekly and Maria was sorry that she had given him such a telling off.

'No, that's not possible,' she said. 'You know he's afraid of him.'

'But he won't even be there, he is going out of town with you.'

'That doesn't matter.'

'Wolf doesn't know what's going on when he's alone.'

'Animals always know what's going on.'

'Why can't I just stay here with Wolf?'

'Just because.'

In the end, she gave in. Lorenz would be allowed to stay at home. With the dog. Walter moaned. Katharina and Heinrich were quite happy. Their brother Lorenz liked showing off in front of them. Especially when other people were around. So they were quite happy for him to stay at home.

Maria sewed herself a blue dress out of the bedroom curtain. She worked on it until her eyes ached. She worked in the night by the light of an oil lamp. She wanted to wear the dress on the trip, set off by the straw hat with the poppy flowers embroidered on it. It was only a few kilometres to L., but still it was an outing. She spun around in front of the mirror in the wardrobe door and was very pleased. She would sit at the front beside the mayor. This image was enough for her.

She wanted to bring back something small for the children. There were always some coins in the sugar jar. She tucked some in her handbag. This was her best one. Josef had given it to her as a present. It had shells stitched along the seams. The clasp was mother-of-pearl. It was sewn together with thread from a material that she did not recognise, a red thread, smooth, shiny and durable.

Maria's sister had married a businessman, who was much older and much richer than Josef. He came from the Rhine valley and had ideas for business ventures. Down in the Rhine valley, more and more farmers were building small workshops on the side of their barns, he told them, and leasing knitting machines. It would not be that onerous, but would bring in a few pennies and they would have a second string to their bow. He, the brother-in-law, wanted to introduce this idea to the Forest. He had discussed this with Josef, back when he had just married Maria's sister. He had made the effort to go and see him up there personally. He rode through the whole Forest on a horse so beautiful that little Walter had wept loudly for joy, and trembled with excitement as Kaspar – that was the name of the man who had sworn to Maria that he would make her sister happy – swung him into the saddle and handed Lorenz the reins so that he could lead the horse with his brother astride it around in a circle. He could really use someone like Josef, the brother-in-law had said, someone who could do calculations; his talent was well known in the Forest. Josef's first word to him was: 'Flatterer!' Wouldn't they all like to move, continued the brother-in-law, from these dismal backwoods where surely there was no future, not for them and definitely not for their children, wouldn't they like to move to L.? Josef should think about his children as well. They themselves already had a telephone and electric light. And the first post van. If that wasn't progress! The brother-in-law had another idea. A crazy idea, said Bella, Maria's sister. Could they not all up sticks and move together to Bregenz! All together! Build a large house! Start up a great business! A new existence! A new life! That had been about eighteen months ago. Kaspar and Bella had been married now for eighteen months and still had no children.

At five thirty on the dot Maria stood in front of the mayor's house with Heinrich, Katharina and Walter, and pulled the bell chain.

The mayor's wife opened the door and clapped her hands together in front of her face.

'When was it we last saw each other?' she sang out.

'Probably about a month ago,' said Maria.

'How can this carry on,' laughed the Lady Mayor, 'you getting twice as beautiful from month to month, Maria. Let's hope the devil is not planning mischief for you!'

Breakfast had already been prepared for the children. The mayor's wife had packed buttered bread and hard-boiled eggs in a tin box for her husband and for Maria.

The mayor wanted to make an impression on Maria. He drove the horses on – two well-fed horses with broad brown backs, the one on the right with a long, light-coloured mane and tail, the one on the left darker with a proud head and more restless. Maria kept a hand on her hat so that it couldn't fly off. She was very aware of how the mayor was edging closer so that certain movements caused their thighs to touch. She pulled her dress tight around her.

'I bet you're a good singer,' he said. 'What's your favourite song? We could sing it together. I sing quite well too.'

Maria, half serious, half joking, said: 'Mary Walked Through a Wood of Thorn.'

'But that's a religious song!'

'It's a round,' she explained to him. 'It sounds lovely when people know it.'

'Right now, I'm not singing any religious songs,' said the mayor.

'Oh well, we won't bother then,' said Maria.

She turned her head away, making out that she had seen something interesting beside the path. The wagon had rubber wheels, that was pleasant and unusual, at any rate in the backwoods. The lane was rough; the fine, smooth paving did not start till the village after next. The mayor stood up briefly from the bench and cracked the reins on the back of the dun, then sat down again, this time closer to Maria as if by pure chance. She had known this would happen. It would be like this both going and coming back. Sometimes he would bend over her, because he had to look at something or other, basically so that he could brush against her again and again, without his intentions being too obvious. If it was limited to this, that would be fine. She was on tenterhooks to see what ruses he might think up that might appear to be unintentional. And whether at some point he might do something more deliberate, that would betray his true intentions. She was not afraid of the mayor. His breath was however off-putting. Too close. Not that it smelled bad. More the opposite. He sucked peppermint sweets. For the very reason that he wanted to smell good. At the same time, it occurred to her that she should be friendly towards him, they were of course expecting quite a lot from him. He wanted to get food supplies for the family and she could ask him for material and thread too. And for shoes. Heinrich wouldn't be embarrassed about wearing shoes from a stranger, his feet were as big as those of an adult. Lorenz, on principle, would not want to put on shoes that someone else had already worn, mainly because it would be nonetheless a form of present, and Lorenz's principle was: I don't want to accept gifts from anyone, so I never have to be grateful to anyone. She wasn't sure about Katharina. She could be obstinate like Lorenz but she loved pretty things, particularly if they also smelled good. Walter liked anything his mother liked. And they needed school things too. School was starting soon.

'Mr Mayor,' she said, 'is it right to sit so close to me?'

''Scuse me,' he said and shifted back.

'It's not important,' she said.

.

'No one needs to call me Mr Mayor,' he said, 'not between ourselves anyway.'

'Gottlieb,' she said.

After a while he commented, 'Gottlieb is the same as Amadeus. Did you know that, Maria?'

'No, I didn't know that.'

'Like Amadeus Mozart,' he said.

'No, I didn't know that,' she repeated.

The mayor had contacts with all and sundry. She could also have asked her sister for things she needed. She would have definitely had all that was needed in abundance. And she would have been happy to give it to her. But then she would have been even more in the position of the poor relation. If I completely reject his advances, she thought, we won't be getting anything. He may give me a kiss on one cheek and do it as if it were a friendly gesture, and he can hold me by the upper arm, no more than that, not too far up, where I'm already sweating under the armpits, and it shouldn't need more than that for him to show a bit of generosity and he won't do more. For myself, I don't want anything.

They drove into the district of L. and already at a distance they could hear the cow bells and music. As a child she had gone to the cattle market every year. That was the time when they had started putting up stalls too, like at a fairground, shooting booths for example, where the lads could shoot at gingerbread hearts, also a stand where they spun

31

sugar candy in three different colours, and open tres-
tle tables, uncovered, where little rings and chains,
bracelets and scarves were displayed, and stands with
cakes and sweet things from the local area – puff
pastry was the highlight for everyone. The visitors
were well-dressed, wearing the best they had. They
were drinking cider. And faces were red even this
early in the morning. A brass band played; there was
one after all. At the back a cymbal, a big drum and
a small drum. Josef had learned to play clarinet as a
child, but had never had one of his own and so gave
it up again. The band played the same military march
three times in a row, until it really got on everyone's
nerves. Then the musicians packed their instruments
away. They would play again in the late afternoon.

The mayor was drinking cider. He had met an
acquaintance. He was holding his tankard up high
for a top-up. Maria was free to have a look around.
You couldn't get lost here, said the mayor. Livestock
stood lined up behind a fence, cows, sheep, goats.
There were three bulls, spotted ones. They had a ring
through the nose and were tied to the ground with
a short chain. Maria couldn't bear to see the despair
in their eyes. Farmers were making deals with each
other in their Sunday best. They clapped their hands
on the backs of the cattle and stroked the calves and
let them lick their hands.

There was a stall with rolls of material. Maria stood
there in awe. All the women in our family do that,

we women love to feel cloth – my mother, my aunts, me especially and my grandmother Maria of course.

'Feel free to touch the material,' said the saleswoman, a Swabian, and Maria took the cloth and rubbed it between thumb and index finger.

'You are not doing it enough,' said the saleswoman, 'you have to really get a proper hold of it.'

Maria wasn't sure what was meant by 'get a proper hold of it'. The saleswoman showed her how. 'First pull up your sleeves,' she said, and she tugged at Maria's blouse, undid the little buttons and pushed the sleeves right up under her armpits, where it was already so damp, 'and then get in there with your arms, as if the material was water. Do you feel how cool it is? That feels so good now that it is getting so hot. You feel sorry for the soldiers, late autumn or spring would be more pleasant for going to war, but now they have to march in the sun in full gear and in Italy it is even hotter than here.'

'Thank you,' said Maria and pulled her sleeves back down again but did not button them.

The mayor was standing behind her: 'Which colour do you like the best?'

'Sky blue,' said Maria.

'Red would suit you better,' he said.

'It doesn't look good on me.'

'But what if it did look good on you?'

There was schnapps too. Would she like to have a small sip, asked the mayor, but he didn't mean it seriously. He liked to drink, but he was never drunk. Most men here seldom drank, but when they did, they got totally legless. Josef never drank at all.

She would go first to her sister and brother-in-law's, she said, and then come back to the market with them.

But that was not her plan. She didn't know what her plan was, the market didn't interest her at all any more. The time would drag until six in the evening. She saw a round, flat lollipop at a sweet stall – it was as big as a side plate, rows of red, white and green spiralling inwards. The salesman said the red was strawberry, the green was woodruff herb, and the white lemon. A huge thing that wouldn't fit in your mouth, let alone the mouth of a child. You would have to break bits off and share them out. But then the lollipop would be destroyed. Even to pick it up was a waste of time. It could be a joint present. One could hang it in the kitchen and whoever wanted to could take a lick. Or Heinrich could have it for five minutes, Katharina five minutes, five minutes for Walter and five minutes for Lorenz, if he wanted. She worried that Lorenz would say, why are you spending money on this rubbish, I don't want a lick. Then he would be the only one that she didn't have a present for. Further over she had seen a little wagon made of wood. Heinrich could pull that along behind him and Walter could sit inside it. But then Lorenz still wouldn't have anything. And what could she get him? Definitely not something to eat, he'd share it with his siblings and give himself the smallest bit, or none of it.

A man came up to her, he was dashing. He was wearing just a white shirt with black trousers, no jacket, and looked like a stranger to the area. He spoke in a strange way, and his haircut was particularly odd, almost bald up to the temples and then a shock of hair at the top.

'Are you looking for something in particular?' he asked.

'Do you have a stall here?' she asked. 'I'm looking for something for my son, he's nine.'

'Well, what things interest him?'

'I don't really know. You talk funny. I've never heard anyone speak that way. What sort of place do you come from?'

The stranger laughed long and hard. 'And I've never heard a woman being so direct.'

'What do you mean by direct?' asked Maria.

'Well, say I had a squint nose and I asked you whether I had a squint nose, then you would most likely say, yes, you have a squint nose. Isn't that right?'

'What else could I say?'

At this, the stranger laughed loud and hard again. This anecdote was told by my grandmother to her eldest daughter Katharina but not until some years later. My Aunt Kathe passed it on to me. She said her mother was drunk only once in her life – she did not know what the occasion for this was – and she had suddenly just out of the blue said she had only fallen in love once in her life, and it was with this man, and from that time she knew that being in love didn't mean much, but love meant a lot. When sober, Maria would never have confided in her daughter like that.

'My name's Georg,' said the stranger and held out his hand to Maria. 'I come from Germany, from the city of Hanover, I am not here just by chance. And you?'

He doesn't want to stare at me, thought Maria, but he is staring at me nonetheless, and he is failing to hide that he is stunned by my beauty. This thought or thoughts in a similar vein had often come to her. It wasn't hard to work out from the stares what men were thinking. He told her that he was here in this village to deliver some sad news to a family. The son of the family had died, a friend of his, his best friend, and it had fallen to him to give the poor people the news.

'Were you at the front when your friend got killed?' asked Maria.

'No,' he said. 'There was an accident, nothing to do with this stupid war.'

He didn't want to say anything more about it, she could tell, but he didn't want to break off the conversation with her, fearing she would then turn and go. Was she from here, he asked.

She gave a short answer. I find this man named Georg attractive, she thought. That was a fact. But she also found the mountains in the evening light attractive. And it wasn't until later that she realised she had fallen in love with him. He mentioned the name of the family he was looking for. It was a common name around here. So she said, no, she didn't know them. They said goodbye with a formal handshake, then she made her way to her sister's, not looking back once, her eyes fixed on the ground. The house stood on an incline. He would be able to watch her all the way up.

Her brother-in-law was in the front garden and called to his wife. She came running out of the house, and the whole kissing and hugging business began. Then they ate bread and ham and drank water with a shot of vinegar in it and sat in front of the house, looking down at the market. At six o'clock, Maria was back down there; there was a lot less going on now that everyone had done the rounds.

'It's time we . . .' said the mayor.

He was in a very good mood and chatted away. He had made an offer for a bull, it would be delivered, he had no need to worry about anything. The purest luxury, a clear profit for everyone who owns a cow. He talked without a break the whole way. He drove through the village and past his own house and didn't let Maria get a word in edgewise, and then made out that he had forgotten that Heinrich,

Katharina and Walter were with his wife, waiting to be picked up.

'I'll send them up. It is still light enough. A bit of exercise will do them good. Then they'll sleep better.'

At the water trough, he helped Maria out of the cart and gave her a package wrapped in brown paper. He had bought some boiled sweets for the children, the stripy ones with a chewy filling, and things for school too. And for her, Maria, an extra package. To show her gratitude, she stood on tiptoe and gave him a kiss, a kiss for Gottlieb, Amadeus. Lorenz sat beside the dog on the steps to the veranda, elbows on his knees, chin in hands, and looked at them.

In the extra packet was some red cloth, with a sheen to it, and with it was some sewing thread.

Then there he was, standing in front of the door. The stranger called Georg. No advance notice. No one had ever given Maria and Josef advance notice of a visit. How would they do it? And why bother? First, send someone to say you are coming and then what? What would be the point? Two trips. One might expect a stranger to ask a lad from the village to accompany him. So that the friendly intention was made clear. Stood all at once in front of her as she was again hanging out the washing, in her hand a white shirt that she had already washed through three times, because her mind was elsewhere – or was it that the clean shirt had smuggled itself into the dirty wash, because it wanted to get rid of the last smell of Josef, because objects know more than people and the shirt knew that Josef would not come back? No, Maria was not superstitious. The stranger just looked at her. Standing, with the shirt cuffs in her hands, arms outspread so that the shirt did not touch the ground. The dog had not uttered so much as a squeak. The man bent down to him, fondled his ear, patted his neck, without taking his gaze off Maria. He looked *right in the innards of her eyes.*

That is an expression my mother sometimes used. If she thought I had been telling lies, she would say: 'Look me right in the innards of my eyes!'

One day I said to her – I must have been about eight and was already full of rage against our family, because I had heard so many stories, particularly about my mother's brothers, none of whom, apart from Heinrich, were like other men – I said to my mother: 'No one else talks like you! You always talk differently from other people! Why do you talk like that, the way no one else does?'

And she said: 'Give me an example! And stop criticising me!'

And I said: 'For example, "look me right in the innards of my eyes". The proper way to say it is, "look me right in the eye" and not "into the innards of my eyes".'

She got that from her mother, she said. 'From your beautiful grandmother.' And continued in the same breath: 'She was just like you.'

I got even more annoyed: 'What's that supposed to mean?' I shouted, stamping my foot. 'See, there you go again. You're always hinting things.'

And she answered: 'Take care you don't end up like her.'

My 'beautiful' grandmother was a role model and a reproach. All the good things were attributed to her, but if my mother did not like something I was doing, she would say I should take care not to end up like her. The good qualities in my grandmother were her gentleness, and that she listened to everyone. She was of the opinion that everyone deserved to be listened to, right to the end, and that only the person speaking could determine when the end had come. Sometimes the thought comes to me that my grandmother's gentleness was in fact indifference and apathy. Another of her good qualities that deserves a mention is that she didn't bear a grudge. The only not-so-good thing about her was her beauty. Not good because of the consequences. In our family, I was considered to be a beauty. No one actually used that word but I had a good idea from all the hints dropped. The hints were, by the way, all in a negative vein. 'You think you can get away with anything just because of your looks!' Or: 'Tie your hair back properly, the last thing you need is to be showing off your hair.' Or even: 'Watch out you don't get like your grandmother!' Looking back, I think my mother had not meant this as a threat. She meant that I should be careful, danger lurks for a pretty face. If that was her intention, she knew the reason why. In the remotest of valleys, it was not in a woman's best interests to be beautiful. That was the implication. In the remotest valley, my grandmother's beauty was talked about even after her death.

I am getting ahead of myself, anticipating something that happens much later in the story, but I can't bear to put it off any longer. I want to speak about it now. At a certain point, the priest turned up at Maria and Josef's house out in that farthest valley, just as unannounced as the stranger called Georg. But the priest was not friendly in the way the stranger was. The stranger was truly friendly. He was friendlier to Maria than anyone who had ever been friendly to her before. Even Josef. He could be tender. When it was dark, very tender even. He was helpful and all sorts of other things. But friendly Josef was not. That was simply not in his nature. The stranger was friendly in a way that made no differentiation between man and woman. The priest, however, just said, without even greeting her: 'Turn your face to the sunlight!'

And Maria did as she was bidden. But asked: 'Why should I?'

'This face gives everything away,' said the priest.

'Like what for example?' said Maria.

'How long has your husband been away?' asked the priest in reply, but it had the ring of an order.

'Since the war began,' said Maria.

'And the belly?'

'What belly?'

'Your belly, you hussy! How long have you had this belly?'

She would have liked to say that she didn't want to be spoken to in that way by anyone, not even a clergyman. But she was so shocked by the vulgar word that she couldn't say anything.

'It's that damned face of yours!' exclaimed the priest. He turned round as he did so, called out to the valley below as if he were at the pulpit and the congregation was down below listening and gazing blankly up at him, women to the right, men on the left. 'Can anyone believe that the Lord God would create such a face? Can anyone believe that the Lord God could be so unjust? The women snivel whenever they see your face and they get on their husbands' nerves. Why not me? That's what they say. As if their husband had made your face himself so that he could stare at it. They come to me for confession, and that's what they say. Why not me? As if I had made your face. Out of what filth then, please tell me? From what filth could I have kneaded such a face? We don't have such filth growing here. Such filth might grow in the city. And then it goes direct from the face to the belly. Ha! That's a short path. One can't even be angry with the men. That's what you're thinking too, isn't it? Answer me, Maria! What are you thinking? Tell me what you're thinking. If I ask you now, you hussy, you would say, of course you would say: whoever, like me, is given a beautiful face by the Lord God – that's what you would say, admit it – to her He gives the right to entertain men. To allow them to approach you. What would be the point of a beautiful face otherwise? This is exactly what you think! Admit it! Admit it!'

This, because my grandmother was pregnant. And Josef was at the front, in the mountain ranges close to Italy. That was when the war was six months old. So it could not have been Josef, thought the priest and probably the whole village. Although he had been on home leave twice. But each time, just a brief stay. The priest and the others reckoned the leave was very short. People started talking as soon as the belly became obvious. Other soldiers' wives were pregnant too, but no one talked about them. Calculations were made and discussed. Leave allowance is three days, fine. Surely a soldier coming home from the front needs at least one day just to rest and is incapable of doing much else? Of course, that's what he needs. So that leaves just two more days. Usually when the man comes direct from war, husband and wife find they have grown apart, that's what people always say, and such estrangement lasts usually even longer than the exhaustion. Let's say, it lasts one day. Fine. Then there is only one day left for consummation of a marriage. And for it to come good on just this particular day may be seen as unlikely. Or at least fairly unlikely.

Maria was pregnant and in her belly was my mother.

My grandmother could not resist the stranger's gaze. Pull yourself together! she told herself. This command was familiar to her in relation to only one thing, and this was lust. There was nothing else in her life for which she had to pull herself together. 'Pull yourself together!' had been something her mother had demanded of her in the past. She had caught her once as she was pleasuring herself by her own hand. And her mother had used the expression, 'by one's own hand'. Later on, Maria had read the phrase somewhere, but in this case it was used to mean that someone had taken their own life. He had died 'by his own hand'. How he had done it was not mentioned. She reckoned it was probably with a knife. You had to hold the knife in one hand, as you cut your other hand, or rather your lower arm. You have to be sure of course not to cut crosswise but lengthwise. Where on earth she had got that from, she had no idea.

'Pull yourself together!' was also the order given to me by my Aunt Kathe. After my mother's death, she was the one in charge of us. 'Pull yourself together!' But she didn't say it when I didn't want to do my homework or when I was being stubborn about something, she said it when she suspected I had a crush on one of the boys again. But Aunt Kathe never said to me that I should watch out that I didn't get like my grandmother.

My grandmother found the man attractive, she had fallen for him. And in fact, the man whose name was Georg was much more attractive to her than Josef ever was. For with Josef there were many other factors in play that were important in a marriage, each of which diluted the importance of the other. With this man it was pure lust.

'I'm married,' was the first thing she said to him.

He said: 'Yes, I know.'

'My husband is at the front,' she said.

He said: 'I'm sorry.' And after a short pause, 'I'm not one of those people who were in favour of the war, not at all.'

'Nor am I,' said Maria.

'Your husband's probably not either,' he said, switching to the familiar '*du*'.

'No, he's not.'

'He can't be so different from you, otherwise you wouldn't have accepted him.'

She felt uncomfortable. Apart from anything else, her arms were getting heavy. She still held the shirt spread out in front of her, as if in defence. With Josef she felt at ease. And sometimes not at ease. In the dark, always at ease. On a bright sunny day, sometimes ill at ease. Because she was slightly scared of him. Now he had gone. One had to reckon with the possibility that he might not come back. Then the story would be, with Josef she had been content, he had been good for her. She had felt content under him. You could guarantee that's what people would say. That's how the women in the village would put it. She had felt content under his body. This was a favourite topic of the women, to imagine the two in bed. The men would put it differently. Josef was of light build. She had often thought of this, when he lay on top of her: my, he's so light. If she had arched her back and suddenly braced herself, he would have fallen off her. He washed himself a lot and very thoroughly. He didn't want to smell like the other men smelled. Of cowshed. For his birthday she had given him some lemon soap. He had been very happy about that. As a young girl, she had felt ashamed of herself, because lust was so important to her, you could probably have seen it in her face. In fact, probably every man could really still see it now. She was what she was. Once she had said in confession to the silhouette of the priest behind the grille: 'I am what I am.' And the priest had answered: 'You just watch yourself!' From then on, she only confessed to having lied a bit or making a face at the Sister a bit or stealing a few apples. Then that priest had died and the new one had come and he had kept an eye on her, a hostile eye, as if she were in league with the devil. Since then, Maria had stopped going to confession.

'How do you know where I live?' she asked, still sticking to the formal '*Sie*'.

'Is that shirt one of your husband's?' asked the stranger in reply.

'I didn't tell you where I live.'

'It looks funny when you hold the shirt out in front of you like that. You don't have to. It looks like . . .'

'What does it look like?'

'No, not funny, sorry. It looks like a city wall. I can't think of another word to describe it. Because I am out of breath from the climb up here.'

'I can't hear you breathing heavily. It's not obvious, not even a bit.'

'I'm nervous. I imagine everyone is when they stand in front of you.'

'I don't know what you're talking about.'

'Everyone here knows where you live. I won't pretend they don't; it might make you wary of me. I would prefer it if we could be on a less formal footing and call each other *"du"*. If you call me *"Sie"*, and I call you *"du"*, it might sound to people like you were afraid of me.'

'There is no one around to think such a thing.'

'I asked someone at the market: where does the friendly woman I was just speaking to live? I forgot to give her something and now she's left, but it's very important. I came all this way just for that, to deliver it. I told a lie, I said I had to bring you a message.'

'Who did you ask?' she said, addressing him as *'du'*.

'A man at a stall who was watching us as we were chatting. He laughed and said he could understand that, with you everyone loses their head and forgets what he actually wanted to say.'

'I don't believe he said that.'

'No, you are right, he didn't say that.'

'Why do you say such things then?'

The man said: 'Don't send me away, Maria. I just want to look at you. I haven't seen anything beautiful in such a long time. I promise I won't come closer than one metre. Just let me look at your face.'

Then there was Lorenz, standing beside his mother. The dog barked, barked loudly. Lorenz grabbed his collar and pulled him away from the stranger.

'Who is this man, Mama?'

The man said: 'I come from a long way away, my name is Georg, like Saint George, who fought against the dragon. A lot of things were laid at my door, let me explain to you. I am not a bad person. I saw your mother at the market. She was friendly to me. It's not often someone is friendly to me. If I was alone with you right now, lad, I would weep as a man weeps in front of another man. But I don't want to weep in front of your mother. How old are you?'

'I'm nine,' said Lorenz, and positioned himself in front of his mother. 'What do you want with her?'

'I lost my best friend,' lamented the man. 'I had to tell his parents. Today I tracked down my friend's parents, but I couldn't bring myself to tell them, I just couldn't get it out. I said I didn't know where he was. I said I came because I thought he might be here. They said he should never show his face there again. He has run off and left us all on our own. He is no longer our son. That's what they said. Though in fact he's dead. And I couldn't bring myself to tell them. Let me come inside, just for half an hour. I am not a danger to anyone. I would just like to sit down for a short while and drink a glass of water.

And Lorenz, despite himself, took a liking to the stranger and invited him into the house and went ahead of Maria, just nine years old he was, and already he acted like the head of the household, though his mother was not happy about it. But Lorenz thought, when Father isn't here, I am the one to decide.

They sat down at the table, Lorenz opposite the stranger so that he had him directly in his sight. Soon Maria stood up again and sorted out this and that, slipped back again onto the corner bench, got up again. She couldn't stay still. The dog had crawled under the table, he lay between Lorenz's feet and the stranger's feet. The cat sat on the window ledge and looked out at the strip of gold white sky still visible above the mountain.

'So are you the eldest?' asked Georg.

'No, Heinrich comes before me, but he doesn't have the wherewithal to deal with people. He is more in tune with animals. I am standing in for my father who had to go to the war. I make sure Mother is all right.'

'Why do you speak in such an odd way? No children speak like that.'

'No one ever speaks the way you speak either,' said Lorenz.

'Around here no one speaks that way; in Hanover, we all speak like that.'

'You talk like writing,' said Lorenz, dropping the formal *'Sie'*. 'That's why I spoke like writing too.'

'What is that supposed to mean?'

'That means,' answered Maria, 'that you use the same language in speaking as in writing. That's what we say around here, someone speaks like writing. Lorenz is good at that.'

'And how do you know how things are written?' asked Georg.

Maria and Lorenz exchanged glances. They didn't know who the question was directed to.

'From reading,' said Lorenz finally.

'What do you read, then?' asked Maria. 'When do you do your reading? I never see you reading. But I believe you. I can understand. You read when you are on your own. I can understand that. He reads when he is on his own. I can understand that.' Then she added: 'I have to go and finish hanging out the washing.'

When the man and the lad were alone, the man told the lad his life story. How he had never amounted to much from childhood onwards, was only ever given the job of cutting leather straps, how he got to know his best friend, whose hands were damaged from the chemicals used in the tannery. He had grown up on the outskirts of the city, everything stank of the tannery day and night, everyone there stank of the tannery even down to their underpants and socks. He and his friend had joined forces, putting their heads together to think up a way they could come by real money. Real money, heaps of it. Not just chickenfeed.

Lorenz said: 'I won't tell anyone, word of honour.'

With a robbery in fact.

'I'm a criminal,' said Georg. 'I attacked a man and robbed him of his money, which wasn't his at all. He was just a courier. But he had a gun with him and we didn't. He pressed the trigger and my friend was dead. And I made a run for it. So there you have it.'

'Did you get away with the money?' asked Lorenz.

Georg bent towards him across the table and whispered: 'Listen lad, could I leave the money with you for safekeeping? I would let you have some of it.'

'How much?' asked Lorenz.

'We can come to an agreement between the two of us,' said the man.

'The story is completely made up, isn't it?' said Lorenz.

Katharina bounced in – the one who would become my strict Aunt Kathe, and so often told me I should pull myself together – and joined them, standing as if posing for a photograph. And pulling along the little wagon with the cat in it was Walter, the one who would become my Uncle Walter, who ran after every woman, unmistakable with his fox-red hair, and who himself was cheated on by his wife with a man who looked like Clark Gable. Sometimes the two of them would take me with them across the border into Switzerland or up into the mountains, where I sat in his car for two hours twiddling the knobs of the radio and getting bored, while they did their thing in a hotel or in a summer meadow. Finally Heinrich came back from seeing to the animals. He would be, as his brother Lorenz said, in tune with animals his whole life. Maria had now finished hanging up the washing outside, and she made coffee and sat down again at her place beside the stranger.

'What are you all talking about?' she asked.

'It's just me and Georg who are talking,' said Lorenz. 'The others aren't saying anything.'

'And what are the two of you talking about?'

Lorenz said: 'Business matters.'

Three children are still to come: my Aunt Irma, my Uncle Sepp, and of course, my mother, Grete. But Grete was the only one to be born while the war was still on.

When I visited the Art History Museum in Vienna for the first time and saw the paintings of farmers by Pieter Bruegel the Elder, I thought to myself: they look just like my people, the people from the stories of my mother and my Aunt Kathe. The children are just like adults, only smaller. They wear the same clothes, just smaller. They have the same serious faces, just smaller. The houses are so small, you can't believe anyone could fit inside them. I know all their stories. They are stories like the ones in the painting about proverbs that I saw in Berlin, in the art gallery of the Prussian Cultural Heritage Foundation. And just as I can't decipher many of the proverbs, I am at a loss to know what to say about many of the stories of my people. Because they are about madness. There is a story about one particular gendarme who, when he had finished his shift, would lie down on the sofa at home and sleep, then eat some Vienna sausages in silence and have a drink of cocoa. Seldom anything different. Then he lay down again on the sofa, until he went to bed in the evening. Never said a word to his wife and children to his death, and when he was home, the radio had to be switched off. His colleagues said that he virtually never said a word at work either. What's going on there with the man in the bottom left-hand corner of the picture? His left foot shoeless, on his right calf a white bandage, he's wearing a white knee-length tunic, with a tightly fitting waistcoat over it that looks like a piece of armour, in his right fist he holds a long knife, unsheathed. He wears a hood on his head and he presses his head against a tiled wall – what kind of proverb does he represent? And what about the beautiful woman just below the centre, the one with the flowing hair, the long purple-red dress with a low-cut neckline, standing behind someone — is it a man, is it a woman — wrapping a cape over his or her head? A broom pokes out of an attic window. There are flat dishes lying on the roof, some empty, some full. Are they actually dishes? A man is leaning forward over a gable roof and shooting with a crossbow at the dishes. Why is he doing that? In the far distance is the sea. There is a story about one young woman, that after she heard the news of her husband's death at the front, she made her way to where her brother and sister lived, two villages away, and didn't get there until forty years later, when the Second World War had already come to an end, in which a son of her sister and a son of her brother had been killed. So many things happen, and happen all in the same moment, even if they happen one after another. Like in the pictures of Pieter Bruegel the Elder.

I have tried it. I can paint a bit. But I never felt satisfied with it. If only I were a musician! The background colours of my prehistory are nearly all shades of brown. Ochre. Cowshed-warm, the colour of cowsheds is brown. Soft. Or frozen earth, icy and iron-hard, with a breath of iron-grey washed over it. One icy morning in January my tongue got stuck on the door handle, frozen to it, and a bit of the skin of my tongue was ripped away. And then sometimes a robe in a blue that made your jaw drop. Hay meadows. Undiluted red seldom, actually never. Buttery yellow. This joy in one moment of sunshine! As if in a game, one was spared from being tagged, just for a while. The colour of the faces indefinable. There is a whole palette of green but the green tends to be hidden. White and black only for Josef. White face, white shirt, black suit and black hair. I used to mix watercolours until the colour matched the skin of my underarms.

Memory has to be seen as utter chaos. Only when a drama is made out of it is some kind of order established. 'That's how life is.' Another saying of my Aunt Kathe's. That's how life is for my family in particular. We never wanted to stand out. Not even my grandmother. But we did stand out. I used to bow my head in shame. I think my grandmother had no chance of not standing out. She takes centre stage. The multitude of the dead lie at her feet. Which does not necessarily mean that they are all roasting in hell. 'We have had everything, and most of it was not granted to us.' Another expression. Who can make head or tail of that, for goodness' sake? Is 'most of it' what we don't actually need to have? My Aunt Kathe used to come out with this phrase, for example, after an evening when they had had visitors, when they had played cards, and eventually someone would get up from the table and say it was time he was going and everyone else would follow him and suddenly the front room would be empty. Aunt Kathe would place her palms flat on the table and say: 'We have had everything, and most of it wasn't granted to us.'

And her husband, the constantly grumpy old grouch, would nod: 'Yes, indeed! Yes, indeed!'

I find myself in this line-up next to my silent mother – she, who when I interrupted my story, had not yet been formed inside Maria's belly. I stand on her heart side. Beside me stands my daughter Paula, who is also no longer among the living. She was the most lively of all of us, as lively as my grandmother. Lively, one hundred years ago, was a sort of reproach. 'Don't be so lively!' That's what they said. 'I'm afraid she's a bit lively' was said as an apology. I can imagine a mother and mother-in-law talking to each other. 'I'm afraid my daughter is a bit lively, says the mother to the mother-in-law about her daughter, nearly adding: 'Unfortunately.' My daughter Paula fell from a mountain at the age of twenty-one, and was killed by a rock. She is with me every day, and all day, as is my mother who died at the age of forty-two, leaving us children behind, the four of us. I was just eleven years old. And three of us were shunted off to Aunt Kathe. My younger brother to Aunt Irma, who like my mother had still not arrived in the world at the point where I interrupted the story of my grandmother.

To bring order to memory – would that not be lying? Lying in the sense that I would be implying that some kind of order exists.

Maria.

She is entranced by the stranger called Georg and can't figure out how it could have gone so far. He sits on the corner bench at the table, he has leant his elbows against the back panelling, this makes his chest seem even broader. He is wearing a new shirt. One that has never been washed. Or at most once or twice. A city shirt. Brand spanking new. She has an eye for that kind of thing. If he has been on the road so long, all the way down from Hanover, she thinks, has he been saving this shirt for special occasions? And he's newly shaven. The men in the village shave maybe twice a week or perhaps only on Saturday. Josef every day. Really, every day. 'I swear to you,' Maria had said to her sister. 'Some days even twice.' Those who are unshaven, those with beards, look unthreatening. Like everyone else really. Josef did not want to appear unthreatening. And not like other people. Black and white was the look he wanted. Black hair, white face. She didn't know where this preference came from. She liked it, she had always liked it.

The stranger was fair, reddish blonde hair. He didn't have immaculately clear skin like Josef, a red patch here, an almost bluish patch there, here a little wrinkle and a scattering of summer freckles everywhere. He laughs his way into the kitchen without a second thought. Points to the salt shaker. Could he have it for his sandwich, he asks, chewing. Admires the small thing. 'It looks like a little man, a hat on top, hands in his pockets.' Maria had been given it by her sister. The pepper shaker has got lost, a little woman. Nothing goes missing in this house, but this piece has gone missing. Salt, the man, pepper, the woman. Georg boxes Lorenz across his upper arm. Stands sideways to him. Laughs with his mouth full. It's nice when someone speaks and laughs at home with their mouth full. Lorenz punches back. Quite unembarrassed. Eleven-year-old Heinrich, old before his time, smiles benignly like a pensioner, that's how he smells too. Maria is embarrassed by how her eldest son smells. Of cowshed, to be honest, and of dried sweat, of an aging body. He could pour water from the trough over his head all day long and scrub himself with his father's fine soap, but he would still smell of cowshed and sweat and old age. And he smelled this way his whole life. And when I was at his funeral, I could have sworn that the grave smelled of him, the wreath, the few flowers, the holy water bowl, the holy water.

Katharina lowers her gaze – can't she find one thing to criticise about the man from Hanover? Does it not occur to her to ask what he is doing here? She likes him, yes, she does. The cat rubs up against his calves, and it headbutts his fist. The dog licks his hand and holds his head out to him, moves it round and round to find the right spot where he would like to be scratched. And little Walter, he is already bouncing up and down on his thighs, the jolly child, who right up until the end of his life will be able to pull the wool over the eyes of anyone he chooses. He could make everyone laugh and never got angry with anyone, not even his wife who cheated on him, not even his lover when she started to take an interest in his youngest brother Sepp, who doesn't appear until much later in this story. With his carroty red hair, Walter would easily pass as a child of the stranger. Can he help Maria with anything, he asks. He has no idea. No, he has no idea. He is unaware of her inner turmoil. Or if he is aware, he isn't taking advantage. Could he have another glass of water? Lorenz pushes forward, takes his glass, runs out and down to the water trough. The man knows I have fallen in love with him, thought Maria, but he's not taking advantage of it.

In love, yes, she was, and it was a better feeling than the one she had for Josef. She had realised this. Again and again. She would never say this to anyone. And what did it matter this feeling, it had no consequences. Georg would not come back again, and she would have nothing from him. Feelings evaporate, only in novels do they last longer, supposedly. In some novels supposedly a whole life long.

When he left in the evening, he laid his hands on her shoulder, they were still inside the house, perhaps someone's eyes might be out on stalks outside. He let his hands lie there for a while, stroking the skin over her shoulder blades with his thumb. He would never trust himself to kiss such a face on impulse, or even if given permission, he said.

And the next day, there he stood in the kitchen again. Maria was just stirring some semolina and milk. She started, and looked at him, and was incapable of uttering a word. The children were somewhere outside the house in the last warm autumn sun. He had allowed for that. There was plenty to do outside, playing games, and building things. The semolina got burned at the bottom, but not too badly. It could still be saved.

'Could I have a taste?' he asked. 'It smells so delicious!'

She stood in front of him and said softly: 'I've been thinking, I hope I can see you again.' She had not had to steel herself to say that. They were already past the point at which saying such a thing would be brazen. But neither of them had been aware of this before.

The children worked outside and pretended they were working, what is playing other than this? But they had seen Georg, coming up the steep path, and they took it for granted, although it was only the second time he had come. My Aunt Kathe told me that this was probably because the children had written off their father, for two of the men who went off to war with him had already died, and so the children probably thought, Mama is looking for another husband, although my aunt couldn't say for certain – in the first place it was too long ago and secondly it had been more a feeling than a thought.

And the day after next he was there again. So early this time that anyone who chanced to see Maria and Georg, out in front of the house after the first breakfast, could have thought the man had been there all night. Lorenz who stepped out of the house behind them still had his nightshirt on, a white one. It was just getting light outside. It was the last day of the holidays, middle of September. But where for goodness' sake could a stranger have slept in that tiny house?

Maria trembled with emotion and when Georg said a 'final goodbye' in the afternoon, she leant her back against the closed door, and he was very close to her – their bodies touching, from the waist belt upwards – and she bit him in the hand. Katharina witnessed it, just as she was opening the door from inside. Georg put his injured hand to his mouth. He swore softly. Then he kissed Maria. And she allowed him to. Transfixed and still and happy. And he could not stop. Katharina watched them.

If I had interrogated my Aunt Kathe, she would have never told me a thing. But one day, when she was already over ninety, she told me. Unprompted. With an expression on her face as if she wanted to get it all out, before it went to the grave with her and was never passed on. She told me about the big kiss. And about the blood that ran into his sleeves, as he held her mother's face between his hands.

Heinrich had not been aware of any of this. He was more in tune with animals, as Lorenz had said, speaking like writing.

I also bit a man's hand, the first man in my life – I met him before I had heard this story. He was married, I was just seventeen. Should I have acted as if he belonged to me alone? Of course, I wanted to be his one and only. His wife doesn't matter. Doesn't count. She is a sort of sister. He speaks about her like a sort of sister. I used to ask after her. 'How is she? Has she got over her cold?' I enquired as if I were worried about her. He was twenty years older than me, had an American car, a 'sled' – over a certain size we would say 'sled', and it was assumed it must be American. He used to park it in front of our apartment building.

My little sister, who knew everything about me and who could hardly remember our mother at all, would look out the window and shout: 'He's here!'

I stood behind her and saw him outside, rolling back the soft top roof and cleaning something with his sleeve from the fin of the sled. He didn't blow the horn. I wouldn't have minded. He didn't want to. He said I ought to keep my ears open and listen out, I would definitely hear when he came. Blowing a horn when picking up a girlfriend was 'tacky'. I didn't know the word and leafed through the dictionary. He did everything by the book. He had a car radio, a Blaupunkt. They were supposed to be the best.

I used to think, I'll let him wait a quarter of an hour, half an hour, until his longing for me rises to a mad crescendo. I was ready for anything. He felt that I wasn't yet.

Half a year later, I was the one waiting for him – in a café, for three hours. I drank black tea until I had stomach cramps. I felt a sad case. I was someone who waited. Constantly waited. I, the one who was born to have others waiting for her! We had a date. I had arrived on the dot. Like every time recently. These little waiting games were getting on my nerves now. He never turned up. Three hours I waited there. The following day, I was back in the same café, I knew that I hadn't got the day wrong but wanted a bit of comfort and pretended that I might have got the day wrong. I even waited again a third day. This time with no illusions. The waitress said: 'Today your tea is on the house.' From her mouth upwards, she was good-looking, expressive eyes, a noble forehead, but her mouth was ugly, her lips slack and downturned.

'There's no point,' she said.

I stopped combing my hair, stopped washing myself, and when Aunt Kathe told me that I looked like a tart on the game, I couldn't care less.

My dearest one – that's what I called him in my thoughts, nowhere else – emerged again six months later and I forgave him and we met up every evening. But one day as he ran his thumb across my mouth, something he had supposedly longed for so avidly during his 'exile', I bit it, and hung onto the base of his thumb like a pitbull terrier, and he screamed and shook my head to and fro. His hand got inflamed and he had a tetanus shot given to him in hospital, which wasn't really necessary – he wanted to show me that I had behaved like a wild beast and that a bite from me had to be treated like the bite of a wild beast.

'How do I explain this to my wife?' he whimpered. 'You can see the tooth marks clearly. The doctor said there'll be a scar, it will look just like the wound. Lifelong.'

I didn't apologise. I suggested he should tell his wife he had bitten himself. To apologise is to admit guilt.

'She would think I was crazy! No one bites themself.'

He should say it was during a dream, I advised, and I swear that I wasn't joking. He should say he had dreamed about a Wiener schnitzel and bitten into it. That would be amusing, his wife would be sure to laugh.

'She won't believe me,' he moaned on. 'She already doesn't trust me. She'll compare my teeth with the imprint! My teeth are completely different from yours!'

'Is that what she's like?' I asked, not in a cynical way at all, I was genuinely surprised. 'The sort who would compare tooth marks?'

His wife lived in Sweden. They had a child that was conceived in Paris. And so this small girl was called Paris, and was seven years old. She lived with her mother in Stockholm and apparently spoke Swedish and German and was super-gifted in other ways. Before he had left, she had announced to him she wanted to read Nietzsche's *Thus Spoke Zarathustra*. He suspected however that she thought it was a novel. I knew the name Nietzsche from my father, and I had heard of the title of the book too but I didn't know whether it was a novel or wasn't a novel. I didn't say anything. He shouldn't get the idea that I, with my seventeen years, was not as bright as his seven-year-old daughter.

'And in spite of everything, I came back to you,' he said.

'How come in spite of?' I asked.

He had come back to me. I wanted to believe all the things he promised me, although I didn't really believe him. He would separate from his wife, he said, this was a rock-solid decision. Divorce would be too complicated. After all, he wanted to be able to hug his daughter every now and then.

I said: 'If you want to separate from her anyway, it doesn't matter if she finds out that I was the one who bit you. She might even sympathise with me and find it easier to let you go.'

He had rented a small apartment in our small town. Of course, he would often be out of town – if that didn't bother me, I could move in with him. Getting married was not a priority, he found marriage hypocritical. He had already lied once in this context and once was enough.

He was friends with the philosopher Karl Jaspers. I asked him, so are you a philosopher too? And he said he was on that track. I didn't know then who Jaspers was. I wrote short letters to my lover, which he liked. He said I had my own ideas and he liked that. And he especially liked how I expressed myself, all in all I was someone special. Once he took me with him to Basel. That's where the philosopher lived. He was not in great health any more, had problems breathing, but he was looking forward to seeing us.

The philosopher looked very old and his voice was soft, and his accent had that sardonic tone that north Germans have, it always sounds to me like they are making a witty remark. I trembled with shyness. I thought, even if I just say, *'Guten Tag'*, I will make some kind of faux pas and be brought up short or ridiculed. My father was an educated man and read the philosophers, so I knew what it meant for me to be meeting one in person. I sat down quietly on the seat that was offered to me. My lover chatted with the philosopher, imitating his way of speaking out of deference. If I remember rightly, the conversation was about 'non-objective thinking'.

At one point the philosopher turned to me and asked how old I was, and then he said he knew me.

'No,' I said, but so quietly that he almost definitely didn't hear me.

'I know a sentence of yours,' he said. He pulled out a slip of paper from under his papers and read: 'I would like to know what you are and why, I can't trust you, everything you want to be sounds invented and you in flesh and blood are probably a cheat and the worst thing is that I don't care . . .'

This was a sentence from a letter to my lover. So he had revealed what was meant only for him. The philosopher looked at me and said, this time without the little north German tone of sarcasm in his voice: 'Please, drink your tea before it gets cold.'

We didn't stay long. The philosopher became tired and we took our leave. Tomorrow evening there would be a party where I could meet interesting people, I should come along. It could be important for my life ahead.

The party took place in an apartment that was stuffed full of books and people, all at least three times my age, the books even older, four times as many men as women. I stood by the wall.

'Don't drink anything, and don't smoke, promise me!' said my lover. And swept off into the crowd. I looked around for the philosopher. No trace of the old man who stole my sentence from me.

A woman came up to me, she had an afro hair style, which in those days was a statement, and she smelled of something sweet, then I didn't know what it was, today I know – patchouli oil, which was also a statement. 'Why don't you come with me,' she said, 'I'll make you a hot chocolate.'

I went up some stairs with her into a small room. It was warm in there, she pressed me down into a sofa and covered me up because I looked so frozen.

'Good you don't smoke or drink, don't let yourself go.' Then she said the sentence which I borrowed from her and coined for my grandmother, 'You probably don't have a chance of not standing out.'

The hot chocolate was very hot and very sweet. She sat down by my side.

'How long have you been together with him?' she asked.

I said that was difficult to answer because between our meetings there were several long gaps.

'You know he's married and has a child with the terrible name of Paris?' She didn't wait for an answer. 'Amazingly, he doesn't tell lies. As far as I know, he has never had an innocent like you before.'

'You don't know anything about me,' I said.

She took me to the station, that very same evening, nudging me onto the pavement in front of her. We walked downhill, she bought me a ticket, held it in front of my face. And wrote a telephone number on the back.

'If you're pregnant, call this number,' she said. 'Ask for me, Heidrun. I'll write it down. It's not an easy name to remember.'

At home the only person that had worried about me was my little sister. In spite of the fact that I had been away for two and a half days. She was lying in my bed, wearing my pyjamas and writing in my notebook. She had thought that I wouldn't come back and that she would have to be me from now on. Later on, when we were both adults, she said she would have liked that.

I know nothing of my grandmother's dreams . . . I inherited just one thing from the beautiful Maria: her sample book. Aunt Kathe gave it to me, one hand laid on it as if she needed to bless it first. The brother-in-law, the worldly Kaspar, had brought it from Vienna. He had had the idea of opening a weaving business in Bregenz, the first in the country, and selling the cloth as far as the capital city in the east. That was before the war. Maria loved fabrics, like me, she couldn't, I can't, keep my fingertips still when silk batiste, tulle, velvet, taffeta, voile lay in front of her, lies in front of me. Even if it is just in the form of small squares in a sample book the size of a child's school bag. When my mother was born, my grandmother lay in a soft bed in her sister's house, the sister who had been present at the home birth and had given my mother an informal baptism, so Maria leant back against the pillow, beside her the tiny Margarethe, Grete, in her little nutshell basket. Maria was Snow White, black as ink, red as blood, white as writing paper. The brother-in-law brought her the sample book, Maria had admired it every time she visited. He said it was a present for her. Maria ran her fingertips over the precious squares and dreamt. Dreamt herself away from everything, away from her family, her children. She would not have felt guilty about it, that's how I see her, that's how I imagine it. As if her family had never existed. As if she had been born in Vienna or in Berlin, in cities where someone like her would be noticed. Her brother-in-law had books with pictures of Vienna and Berlin that she liked looking at. She daydreamed about being at the opera, looking down from a box into the audience, and noticing how people were whispering about her. She was the beauty being talked about. It was a place for fine ladies to see and be seen and she was one of them. She wore an ice-blue dress, an ice-blue matching the crusty snow that twinkles when the sun hits it, and she had eyes as bright as the heroines in novels. She would conceal her washer-worn fingers with gloves of Atlas silk. Or no, she wouldn't have worn fingers at all! She would be a city girl, born and bred. Would she have a beau at her side? Would the word 'beau' sound the same to the city women as it did to her? Or would they find the word comical? Sometimes the beau in her dream resembled Josef, at other times Georg. Josef was more distinguished all in black, but it was Georg that made her heart pound. Josef in a formal suit would be the most handsome man at the opera. Everyone's gaze would be on him. In a dream one can be self-centred. She didn't want to share the admiration with anyone. She wanted to be admired, just her alone. So she saw Georg at her side. She might call him tenderly 'my fox' because of his temperament and his colouring. They would drive home in their carriage to their city apartment and in her excitement, the 'shampane' glass would fall over. She didn't even know how to spell the word 'Champagne'. Georg would pull her dress up over her head, she would be a bit dizzy from the alcohol, and Georg would have a bath run for her. It would be like in the Orient. She would not be worn-down. As she climbed out of the steam, it would look as if she were stepping directly out of a cloud. Georg would say: 'I have never seen anything so beautiful anywhere in the world.' One daydream, one minute, and already crushed. I am the one inventing and writing down this dream and I believe in it longer than Maria. I know nothing of the dreams of my grandmother.

And then Georg did come back once more. But this time, he did not see Maria. Lorenz had intercepted him down at the water trough. He was working on his invention down there and wanted to tell Georg about it.

About the problem with the water, in fact. The water storage tank was slightly below the house and did not even belong to them. But the person to whom it belonged had never been in touch. The stream flowed down from the mountain. Before Josef and Maria's time, someone had fixed a wooden runnel, and water was diverted off from the stream and fed into a concrete-lined trough. It was a good one and a half metres wide, and the same in length, and about one metre high, probably intended for the cattle. Josef had nailed together some planks to make a cover. The last section of the runnel was moveable, so that the water could either be directed into the basin or left to flow alongside it. If one knelt down in the trough, one could have the water flowing over one's head. It was of course extremely cold. This is how Josef washed every day. Naked from head to foot. Even in winter, as long as the stream hadn't frozen over. The water that was required in the house had to be carried up in buckets. A very unpopular task. Lorenz wanted to invent a solution. In the first place to make the life of his mother, his siblings and himself easier, but more because he got great pleasure from puzzling out such things: how could this work? He had already seen at his aunt's house how nice it was to have running water and electricity.

As Lorenz sat at the edge of the water trough and pondered, letting his imagination fly, he saw Georg coming up the gravel path. He ran to meet him and by the time they both arrived back at the trough,

Lorenz had already explained his idea: a kind of rope pulley with hooks attached to it, on which the buckets could be hung. One person stays down by the tank and fills the buckets, above is another person who turns a sort of crank.

'When someone says "a sort of", they haven't figured out exactly how,' was Georg's comment.

At this, Lorenz fell silent.

'Do a drawing,' said Georg.

Lorenz remained silent.

'Don't be offended,' said Georg and he said he had come to say goodbye for the last time. But he had a suggestion for him – when the war was over and everything was back to normal and his father had returned safe and well, and Lorenz had finished his schooling, would he not like to come to Hanover? 'I will find you a good opportunity. People like you need to move to the city. That's where they're needed. Here in the country, who needs people with ideas?'

Georg pulled a leather pouch out of his pocket and handed it to Lorenz. 'Hide it,' he said, 'and if your mother gets into difficulties, give it to her.'

'What happened to your hand?' asked Lorenz.

Georg had bandaged it up. Katharina had not told anyone what she had seen. Because she could not make head nor tail of it. Why is Mama biting the man's hand? Why is she doing that? But she likes him. Everyone likes him. You don't bite someone that you like.

'That's the least of my troubles,' said Georg. 'It's getting better.'

Then he had stood there for a while at a loss, looked up to the house, held his healthy hand in the stream of water, and said that it really was very cold. No one was up at the house. He had inhaled deeply once more and was gone.

My Uncle Lorenz respected the request. He kept the pouch with him, hidden under his things, asked himself every time his mother got into difficulty whether this was the moment, and did not open the pouch until both she and his father had passed away. But there was no money in the pouch, no gold either, although from the outside it had felt like it. There was a handful of lovely stones inside, a large piece of quartz, half a dozen shells and a sea snail. And among these, a piece of paper, folded over several times. On it was written: 'My Love'.

Lorenz gave his mother the news and said Georg would not be coming any more. He had asked him expressly to say these exact words and had expressly asked him to pass them on to her. She waited until it was night and the children were asleep, and then drank the schnapps that was supposed to be for cleaning wounds, drank the whole bottle. Katharina found her early the next morning and thought she was dead. She ran just as she was, her hair loose, in her nightdress, in the dark, barefoot, down to the mayor, banged with both fists on the front door and shrieked that the most terrible thing had happened.

The mayor lifted up Maria and carried her down to the water tank. There, he undressed her and placed her in the concrete trough and let the cold water run over her until her skin turned blue. He dried her off with his shirt and carried her naked back into the house. He wrapped her in a blanket and laid her on the bed. Then he waited with Katharina until it got light. The child and the man sat in the kitchen, the door to the bedroom open. There was no need for her to go to school today, he said. Lorenz and Heinrich as well. He sent Katharina off down into the village to his wife. She should come up and bring a hearty breakfast for everyone. Especially some bean coffee. Ground.

But that was not the end of it. The despair had not played out yet, one could only wonder where such despair came from.

What is it with those thoughts that lurk at the back of the mind? They lie low under the surface and await their moment. They are patient but as soon as they spot a chink, they launch themselves into the main narrative and change everything. Georg had hoped the story might go like this: if Maria's husband did not return from the war, he, Georg, would take on the whole family and be its devoted head and move with all of them to Hanover. First consulting each one, one after the other, asking did they really want to go. And if not, then they wouldn't. They would stay here. He wasn't some kind of dictator. But not staying in the small house at the end of the valley, definitely not there. Something else would turn up. Those were the ideas at the back of Georg's mind.

Lorenz sensed these thoughts. But pushed them aside. He liked the man, really liked him, he could quite easily imagine spending the whole day with him. He had never been able to do this with his father. Lorenz liked chatting, his father didn't. A man who has a dip every day even in winter, cold water running over his naked body, was not like other men. And if such a man almost never utters a word, his son cannot fathom much about him. He could not even tell whether he loved Mama. With Georg he could see it clearly. Lorenz did some heart-searching: am I as fond of my father as I am of Georg? Had his father ever spoken to him about an invention? No, this he had not. And never would.

All that remained under the surface.

What happened under the surface was more intense than reality. Maria had not seen that Georg had visited once more. Lorenz had had a look on his face though. Guarded. The look on his face seemed to betray that he was hiding something. She gave him a grilling and he admitted it. Mother raced out. She swept the crockery from the table and, in the night, when she was alone, she drank the whole of the schnapps bottle down to the last drop. And collapsed on the kitchen floor. And Katharina found her mother. And so on, I've told this part already. Actually, I should tell the story three times, one after another. That's what my Aunt Katharina did, when she eventually got round to telling the story. She told the story from beginning to end three times. The same, word for word, starting with Lorenz down at the water trough, how he sees Georg climbing up, then to the part where Lorenz has a look on his face, how Mother grills him, how she races out, how she drinks the whole of the schnapps bottle down to the last drop, and how she, Katharina, runs down to the village, to the mayor, and then down again to the mayor's wife. She told the story in a repetitive monotone right to the end, told how the mayor had carried her naked mother up from the water trough and laid her on the bed and covered her with blankets, and how he had sent her, Katharina, down into the village to his wife, to get her to come up with some coffee. And when my aunt had finished, she started again from the beginning, without a pause, and did that in total three times. No commentary. I was to make of it what I would.

That actually Maria did not want to live any more from that day onwards. And that if she had died, I would not exist, for Grete, my mama, had not yet been born. That was another thing I should think about.

Once Maria was sober again, she was ashamed of herself. She kept her eyes shut. She tried to think up an excuse. She wanted to say she had dreamt that Josef had been hit by a bullet, and that she had had a momentary fit of madness, and this madness had led her to drink the schnapps. But it all sounded too stupid. So she kept her eyes closed and played dead, let her breath out very slowly for as long as she could. The mayor's face was bent over her, she smelled the peppermint. He stroked her cheeks.

Little Walter, Lorenz and Heinrich were standing at the side of the bed.

'Someone has to call the doctor,' said the mayor. 'He needs to have a look at her, she probably has alcohol poisoning. He needs to pump that stuff out of her stomach and her insides.'

Heinrich needed to run and follow Katharina into the village and tell the Postadjunkt to telephone the doctor. In all the excitement, he had forgotten to say this to Katharina.

Heinrich looked down and didn't respond, he was afraid he would do something wrong.

Lorenz stepped forward: 'I'll go,' he said, and to the mayor, 'but you stay with her!' addressing him with the familiar *'du'*.

'I will, I promise you,' said the mayor, as if Lorenz were a grown-up, as if he were his own father.

Lorenz knew some drunks from the village, all of them men, who staggered around at the weekend and fell over and often lay where they had fallen until the following morning. But could a woman survive that? His father had never been one of them. His father drank no alcohol. Lorenz knew there was a rumour about a woman who once drank too much and drowned in the cesspool with her newborn child. She had drunk a full bottle of schnapps. Mother had said about her at the time, the poor woman, she couldn't cope with it all any more. There was also the expression, 'Did it get to you?' This is what they said, when someone did something that one would never have believed of them. 'It got to him.' What got to him? As if an animal had got him. That's what it sounded like. Did it get to Mother?

The mayor sent Heinrich out of the house. 'And take Walter with you. He doesn't need to see all this! You go with him. Go up the mountain with him for an hour, and stay an hour more after that!'

The doctor did not come until the evening. He said that it would all be fine. Nothing to worry about. Just a major hangover.

The children took on their mother's tasks as she needed rest for her recuperation. The mayor visited her every day until the colour came back into her cheeks again. It took much longer than if it had just been a hangover.

The mayor had observed the stranger going up to Maria's house three times. He didn't know whether anyone else had seen. The Postadjunkt perhaps. The postman would never say anything to anyone. He would never say anything that could harm Maria. When the mayor visited Maria, he would sit down opposite her in the kitchen, she was still very pale. He felt he had the upper hand, he gazed at Maria like he had never done before, and stroked her across the neck, which he would never have done in this way before. He would grasp a strand of her hair and wrap it around his hand and pull her towards him, that was all new. Maria did not protest.

The mayor said: 'Maria, don't you think you should give yourself a wash again? You always used to be so clean, and your things were always so white.'

Her blouse had stains, the children's shirts had not been washed for ages. Katharina swept the floor, Lorenz washed and sorted the crockery, Heinrich as always looked after the cowshed, but in general the place was a mess.

'Who was this man? Who was he?' asked the mayor. And as she did not reply, he asked again. Then he shouted out, swung his arm back, made a punch in the air. He wanted to punch the air and act out hitting the man. The mayor was not one for fighting. But he could see the problem.

'Was he pestering you?'

Maria did not reply.

'Did you enjoy being pestered by him?' And he changed his manner of speaking, as if he was suddenly in Maria's house in an official capacity. Had she enjoyed it?

The mayor had been asked by Josef to look after Maria and he had promised to do this, and this was how he thought he should do it.

'Explain to me,' said the mayor, and no longer stroked her tenderly on the cheeks but grabbed her by the shoulder. 'Explain the situation to me!'

And as she still did not answer, he yelled at her, and jumped up forgetting everything his own mother had taught him about decent behaviour: 'And don't lie to me, woman! I've come to the end of my patience, damn you! Now I see through you! Poor Josef! Everything is a lie with you. Always, everything is a lie with you. So many lies, you could buy a car with them and ride around the whole valley, a black motor car with a Swiss number plate and everyone would think it belonged to a Swiss millionaire. Was he Swiss? Tell me! Was he Swiss, I'm asking you! Did he give you money? Show it to me! They are grabbing everything for themselves, ducking out of everything and grabbing everything for themselves.'

And the mayor shook Maria again by the shoulders, gripped her shoulders and her back. She pressed her hands to her face and wept, and that made the mayor even more furious.

'So now you're weeping for him? That tells me everything! She's weeping for him, that tells me everything!'

The next day the mayor came back up the mountainside, knocked and said through the gap in the door he was sorry, would Maria please forgive him? He had forgotten all that his mother had taught him about decent behaviour, but it was only because he was so worried about her.

My grandmother recovered. Did not speak about the past. When the moon shone into her bedroom, she lay awake and thought of Georg. How deeply he had rooted himself into her heart! No one could deprive her of her longing, because thoughts are free. She knew no one she could trust. The mayor came every day and said he would see her right. He had not managed to find out who the man was. Lorenz had told him that the man came from Hanover and his name was Georg. He knew nothing more. Mother had got to know him on market day. When asked how often he had visited Maria, Lorenz said that he knew of only two occasions.

A letter came from Josef announcing a period of leave from the front.

Two of his comrades had fallen right at the beginning. Also two of those who were called up later. Four dead from the village. This was communicated to the wives or to the mothers respectively by letter. The priest had preached in church about the dead. Lorenz had said to his mother that she was expected to go to church this time, as she had not gone at the time of the first deaths. Maria and the children sat down in a pew at the back, Heinrich, Lorenz and Walter too, all together on the left-hand side of the altar, Our Lady's side. She had Josef's letter with her in the beautiful handbag he had given her, the one with shells along the edges and the mother-of-pearl clasp. As if the letter was a guarantee of survival. There was not a single tender word in it. But she knew what to make of that.

What did Maria know of her handsome soldier? Nothing. What did she know about the war? Almost nothing. Except that the women left at home were scared. People had reckoned on the men being back home again by the autumn. And then two were dead at the beginning of September and then another two in November. When Maria thought of her husband, the first thing that came to mind was his obsession with cleanliness. He would be unhappy in the dirt. Obviously, in war it would not be possible to splash water over one's head every day, that much was clear. And always the same shirt and certainly not white. And as scratchy as sandpaper. And would he be able to clean his teeth? Would a man like her husband, such a clean person, be laughed at in his attempts to keep clean? She could not imagine that Josef would be laughed at. Would he clean his teeth with salt, even at the front? His fellow soldiers, what did they look like? Did they stink? No clean underwear. No bar of lovely lemon soap, only available from the mayor.

But she didn't want to think about the mayor. He had unbuttoned her blouse, eleven buttons, to reach her breasts while making veiled threats to her, how would Josef take it if he learned about the man from Hanover? And Maria had shut her eyes and waited. He had put one hand on each of her breasts. And then he had groped behind the waistband of her skirt, not all the way down, because she had blinked. That had sufficed. Blinked and the mayor took fright, jerked his hands away behind his back. The things I have to put up with, thought Maria, just so we can get gifts from him to make our life a bit easier and so he holds his tongue.

History means: it is over. Josef would lie wordless next to her in bed and she would sit astride him and wait for him to finish. Josef, the father of her children – she would stay with him until the day of her death. What she did not yet know was that day would not be long in coming.

He was not in the field; he was in the mountains. His battles were taking place in the mountains. They had dug out caves for themselves, in Italy. They lived in the mountains as if in houses. There were tables, benches, camp beds, curtains if someone wanted some time alone. It was draughty. The caves were like chimneys. And it was almost always noisy. And the filthy language they used, it got on his nerves. Josef did not avail himself of that, never had done, even at home.

He had earned money, 'in the field', in the mountains. By what means and methods he did not say. He laid a roll of banknotes on the kitchen table in front of Maria. Wrapped in a pair of underpants.

He wanted warm water and soap, only then would he lie down with his wife. Maria spread a hand towel out on the kitchen floor, he stepped onto it. First he scrubbed himself down with the hot water, Maria scrubbed his back, then he snipped his toenails and fingernails and filed them, then he shaved and lathered himself again and shaved a second time. His hair had been cut recently, especially for his leave, at least that service operated properly in the camp. That and a couple of other things. All at once, Josef opened up. But only for a short while. As if a water tap had been turned on and then turned off again straightaway. He put the hand towel across his shoulders and ran naked and barefoot down to the water tank and sat down in the concrete trough. On All Hallows' Eve it had snowed and the snow was still lying in places. Cold had never bothered him.

In bed, close to his wife, Josef found it difficult not to think of the men, the two from the village, who had been shot – he had only just found out about them from Maria – and about the other two as well. They had not been together, he and the men from the village. One had been sent here, the other went there; the very day after they had left the village, they had been separated. Their hats had lasted longer than their heads. So four were already dead.

His body was cold. It was as if there was no warmth in him, right into the depths of his being, as if even the blood in his heart was cold. He was the remaining survivor; he should have a guilty conscience, so he said. And that was about all he said about the war.

'And do you?' she asked.

'If I had anything to do with it, there would be no war,' he said. But he knew that everyone in the village expected a guilty conscience of him.

'How do you know?' she asked. She for one had not heard anything of the kind.

In the field, people talked about these things, he answered. Then he said: 'There is still no guarantee I will survive. You're right. I don't need to have a guilty conscience, until the final reckoning has come.'

She preferred not to say anything to this.

'Why do they call it "in the field"?' she asked and had no idea why she asked this; it did not interest her in the least.

'The top brass thought that one up,' he said. They also said 'fallen', as if dying out there was simply falling down. He at least had not seen anyone simply fall down. He could tell them a thing or two about how men died out there. No question of a mere 'falling down'. How did they think up such rubbish! Again, it was as if the water tap had been turned on. One minute standing, next minute fallen. What rubbish.

Most of the time when shooting is going on, you are lying flat, and if something hits you, then you just remain flat out on the ground. Then the tap was turned off again. Maria was not used to these sudden outpourings from her husband. They made her feel uneasy. They were a sign to her that he had changed. She was apprehensive about what else might have changed in him.

She thought, it's the bad conscience that makes his body so cold. She snuggled up against him, rubbed his back, his backside pressed against her lap.

'I just can't get you warm,' she said.

'I don't feel cold,' he said.

If you had only seen this madness. If you had only seen the field hospital. Everyone wanted to get into the field hospital. Because everyone thought there were beds there with clean sheets. And a bathtub. A bathtub! And scented soap. Scented soap! But after one visit, they were hankering to get back to the front. In comparison, their draughty cave was positively cosy. Once you had smelled the stench in the hospital. When you had seen the arms and the legs. They lay around. As if someone had forgotten them. They just lie around. And there are other things lying around as well.

'What else lies around?' she asked.

'You don't want to know,' he said.

'Well, we don't need to talk about that,' she said.

'Yes, better not,' he said.

They were silent. As if there was nothing else to speak about. He hadn't even asked once after the children. And now she came to think of it, he hadn't even had a proper look at them yet.

She said: 'The children are well.' As if he had asked about them.

'Yes,' he said.

Lorenz had reached out his hand to him like a stranger. Heinrich copied Lorenz. Only Walter and Katharina had flown into their father's arms. Katharina wanted to play the string game with him right there and then, she held a loop of string firmly between her fingers and said he should take it from her. Maria showed him how it was done and he did it. He still had his rucksack on his back and had not even stepped inside the house.

'The amputated limbs,' he said.

'Better not,' she said.

But he carried on talking, was still cold, just his hands, they were warming up gradually. He had placed them between her legs, he stroked her pubic hair.

'The gunfire victims . . . one evening they sang a song together . . . can you imagine it . . . each one had something missing . . . one of them half his jaw . . . that he could still sing . . .' That was when he wished he was back at the front.

'Why were you in the hospital, for God's sake?' she asked. 'You didn't get shot, did you?'

He'd had a fever. The broken tooth. In the field everything got inflamed so quickly. There were people who died of a mere scratch. And in dreadful suffering. If nothing is done to prevent it, you die more quickly than you might think. It would be shameful to die in the field of a toothache. Even people in the village would get to hear of it.

'Has the tooth been taken out?' she asked.

'Yes,' he said. 'I'll show it to you tomorrow.'

'One quite near the front?'

'No, right at the back.'

'Are they able to do that in a field hospital?'

'Actually, they are the best,' he said. They were the best at everything. Where he was, they were the best. The best soldiers, the best barbers, the best teeth extractors. They were mountain infantrymen. There was no one to beat them. Even the emperor said that.

'People will talk about us for many a year,' he said.

Then he fell asleep. Mid-sentence. Maria shortly afterwards. In the night, both of them woke up at the same time. Then between them, it was as if the war did not exist. And as if the man from Hanover had never existed. Maria said it had never been as good for her before. He said it was the same for him. They made love again in the morning.

'How long have you got?' asked Maria.

He said: 'Four days. Perhaps less.' Then he said: 'It's strange that you haven't asked till now.'

'Strange that you haven't told me till now,' she countered.

They agreed that this was because they loved each other so much and so the war had been brushed to one side. But this was not the case, not for her, not for him. When he laughed, she could see the gap in his teeth. It looked rakish. She liked it. The war had made her Josef even more handsome. Imagine that!

Mayor Fink, Gottlieb, had come to visit again. He clapped Josef on the shoulder so heavily in greeting that Maria saw the rage mounting in her husband's eyes, and she was afraid something would happen at any minute that she would not have thought possible before Josef was called up to war. She knew that he was quick to anger, but hitting someone was not something he had ever done before. Perhaps he had learned this during the war. But nothing happened. The Italian troops had of course suffered losses, thank God, said the mayor, but they had the advantage in numbers unfortunately.

'That God business is a bit of an issue anyway,' he said. But there was no more discussion on the matter.

Then, through the window, Maria spotted her husband talking with the mayor. They're talking about me, she thought. Josef gave the mayor something wrapped up. Bank notes again probably, thought Maria. This time not wrapped in underpants. That she had a husband who understood how to do deals even in wartime, that was something she could be proud of. She remembered what her brother-in-law had once said – he was surprised that Josef had not made more of himself. He was wearing his Sunday suit, she only noticed it now. She laughed to herself. Because their lovemaking in the night and in the morning had been so good, he had put on his Sunday suit. And now he would be asking the mayor whether his wife had been faithful. Supposing the mayor told him about the visit from Hanover, and lied that he had found him in the house so early in the morning, yes, inside the house, so early that you might wonder if he had perhaps spent the night here, supposing the mayor told him that, then . . . Josef was unarmed when he came home from the war, however he had probably killed many Italians in the mountains.

The mayor stuffed the wrapped packet into his pocket, he hadn't examined it. Maria felt as if what was in the packet represented her value. Her price. A certain amount had to be paid when she was given back unsullied. She was disgusted and at the same time proud.

No one in the family wanted their father to lift a finger, he was there to rest. Josef did what he had done before the war. He went into the cowshed. He praised Heinrich. Heinrich worked at his side. He praised Lorenz too. Little Walter ran into the cowshed and his father lifted him up onto the best-looking cow, all in his Sunday suit. It would take her a whole day to clean the suit and three days to air it.

'Do you have cows in the war too?' asked Walter.

'Horses,' said Lorenz, and Father nodded.

The mayor came a second time. He sat down with Josef. As far as Maria could gather, it was about business. Perhaps it had been about business back then outside the front door, and not about her at all. The mayor smelled of schnapps. Maria served them both with the gifts from the mayor. Cider, bacon, cheese. Then she went into the bedroom and pinned up some flannel for a new shirt. Josef could wear it under his rough military gear. And against the cold in the mountains. That would do him good. He might remember how he had warmed his hands between her legs. He was after all her husband.

The kitchen was the only warm place. In the mornings, there were already frost flowers on the windows, and if one wanted to see out into the world, one had to scratch.

Josef went back to the war. He had to go back again after just three days. They promise you four days and give you three. It snowed. Maria watched as he walked down the path to the village. As if he were going to march all the way through to Italy. On his back, the grey rucksack that belonged not to him but to the emperor.

Aunt Kathe told me that in the war Father had forgotten how to kiss and cuddle. Kissing and cuddling in public had never been his way and according to him in public meant anywhere outside the house. Even if no one was to be seen for miles around. If someone came up the path, you could see him at least a quarter of an hour before you heard his voice or he heard a voice from above. Nevertheless, when Father stepped out of the house, kissing and cuddling and caressing stopped. The door marked the boundary of being in public. When he came home from the war, he didn't kiss and cuddle any more, even inside the house. She, Katharina, had wanted to hug him and kiss him, he had turned his head away and fended her off with his hands. What happened between Mama and Papa in the bedroom, she had no knowledge of that of course. She had been hurt that her father had pushed her away. It was never the same, the relationship between her and her father, as it had been before the war.

'To be blunt,' she said, 'I lost my Papa in the war. Before I used to call him Papa and after the war I called him Father.'

'So?' I asked. 'What did he say to that? That all of a sudden he was Father and not Papa any more.'

'Yes, you're right,' she said. 'I'd forgotten. It's true, he did say something. Now that you ask, I can see him in front of me. And I can hear his words again. It's fascinating how one's memory works.'

'Well, what did he actually say?' I asked again.

'He said . . . he said. Hey, you've become a cold little creature. That's the funny thing. He would never have said such a thing before the war. Not in that way.'

'You're not a cold little creature, Aunt Kathe,' I said.

'Yes, I am, I am,' she said.

My Aunt Kathe, a woman no longer quite so young, once had a suitor, but one that she was not keen on. He came from a working-class family and boasted about the fact that when he was fourteen, he had knocked his father flat out under the table, up till then it had been the other way round. In addition, he had citizenship in Liechtenstein. Which for him meant he could get away with pretty much anything. My aunt hated violence. The suitor did not give up, he threatened to kill her if she did not marry him. Kathe believed him and became his wife. She thought, the way I look, no one else will ever be interested in me, so I'll just go for this one. Her husband was harmless, but only to her. He was strict and cruel to his sons. He was indifferent to his daughter. When one son lost his watch in the gym, he took the strap from the kitchen cabinet and beat him almost to death. This son had a friend that he liked to play cards with. I liked this friend a lot because he said to me that I would definitely become something special, one hundred per cent definite. I wanted to play cards with them both and they let me, but if I 'shot a buck' – that meant 'made a blunder' – I would have to crouch under the table. Aunt Kathe's husband was made of skin and bone. He ate nothing, drank ten beers every evening. He used to send me to the kiosk to fetch 'Dreier', the cheapest brand of cigarettes without filters, packed in a carton. Be careful with the carton, he used to say, if you shake it around, the tobacco drops out, then you'll get what's coming to you. I shook it around but never had anything coming to me. After the death of our mother, my two sisters and I lived with Aunt Kathe. She had taken us under her wing in her three-bedroom apartment, in the South Tyrolean Settlement – a development where the poor people lived. We shared the small amount of breathing space with her, her two children, her husband, her brothers, Walter and Sepp, and one of her nieces. Every morning, even in the bitter winter months, she used to stand by the open window to show us physical exercises that we had to copy. I was really good at it but was never given any praise. She sewed sleeve protectors for us but I always took mine straight off again and shoved them in my schoolbag. She tried to be fair. We were afraid of her irascible husband, but he paid no attention to us. He listened to the news at the top of every hour and if one of his sons said as much as a single word, he shouted him down and hit him on the fingers with a fork. Auntie also took in two of her brothers who had separated from their wives, Walter and Sepp. She was a better cook than any top chef. She said she couldn't make me out and that was a problem and would be a problem my whole life long. My little sister was only four years old and wet the bed if she was not taken to the bathroom in the night. But our aunt's husband had forbidden that. So my older sister and I sat on her bed and implored her to urinate into the large milk jug, but the child didn't want to. In the evening, Auntie would put all the shoes by the front door. I sat on the doormat and polished them, I loved doing it, because you could see a result.

When Aunt Kathe lay in her coffin surrounded by hibiscus flowers, she looked like an old American Indian woman.

The mayor did not suffer from self-doubt. Since becoming mayor, he scrubbed his hands every day, mixed some sand with the soap powder, picked out the dirt from under his fingernails with his pocket-knife, shaved first thing in the morning and splashed himself with eau de cologne. A politician, he used to say, and a mayor was clearly a politician, had to make the correct decisions, even if sometimes they were not 'good', good in the sense of the catechism. Nature, one didn't have to have studied it, is not good, just take a look at it, but it is always in the right. When he lay next to his wife, whom he honoured in accordance with all the laws, he thought about Maria and imagined what it would be like if she were lying naked beside him. He had seen Maria naked. When he had carried her down to the water trough, held her under the water and brought her up again to the house. He felt it was greatly to his credit that he had not taken advantage of her weak state. That the thought of taking advantage of her had not even occurred to him. Or was it possible, he wondered, that Maria actually wanted someone going up there, someone who would take advantage of such a situation? And that the rogue from Hanover was such a one? He could see the two of them in the bedroom. Lie down, said the man, and the woman lay down. Undo your buttons, said the man. And the woman undid her buttons. Spread wide, said the man. Had there never been anyone in her life up till now who had made advances to her in that way? Maybe that's why she drank herself silly when he left, because she was afraid no one like that would ever come to her again.

The mayor had managed to convince Josef during his home leave of the faithfulness of his wife. Josef had said just one word, as they stood alone in front of the house: 'And?'

The mayor had made out as if the question mark related to the free supply of provisions, as if the idea that he could be referring to anything else was unthinkable. 'We have plenty to spare,' he answered. 'Every second day I brought things up for her and the children. It comes from the heart and I speak for my wife as well. No need for thanks.'

And he got no thanks either.

Josef asked yet again: 'And?'

Then the mayor pulled a face, as if he had just worked out what he meant, and grinned companionably: 'No one messes with me. And they all know that if they ever stepped out of line, they would have to reckon with *me*. And they all know what that would mean.'

Josef was still not happy with the answer. And he added a second word to the first: 'And her?'

The mayor carried on the game: 'And her? What do you mean?'

'Her!' repeated Josef severely, in a recently acquired tone of command.

'Ah, you mean Maria!' called out the mayor. 'If Maria? From her side?' And he played his role so well that he got genuinely angry. 'What has happened to you in the field, Josef? My goodness! This is what war does to people? Have you forgotten what your wife is like? Josef! I could always have vouched for her and in fact I did tell you that before you left. You don't need me checking up on her. You might need me as a protector but not for checking on her. No one needs to check on her. Only when someone is thinking of straying from the path. That's when I am needed. But no one thinks of doing that. Because no one wants to mess with me. You can rely on Maria one hundred per cent. Has it got to the stage where I know your wife better than you do? Josef!'

Josef nodded and was reassured. On following leaves from the front he would not ask again. If there were to be any more. Or perhaps there would be no more. For whatever reasons. Cold, snow and avalanches were worse enemies than those Italian chestnut chompers. But even a bullet from the gun of a coward can hit you, a stray shot too.

When the mayor had been alone with Maria, he had heaped praise on her. How she had kept the family together, raised the children, kept the house clean. All on her own. He had run his finger over surfaces and held his finger up to her eyes and exclaimed: 'Nothing. Not a speck of dust!' She had just smiled at this. He knew no other woman with such a beautiful smile. Above all though, he knew no other woman who sat so beautifully. Although all of her was good to look at, when she was sitting down – her firm breasts even more prominent, because she was sitting upright, the hollow of her back, the rounded hips, because they were more rounded as she was seated, her smooth, graceful neck, a long neck because she held her head high – and although this was so, and although it was enough to make any man crazy and reckless, he felt a tenderness for her, and he thought: it's better I leave her alone. When she was sitting, he felt this tenderness more than desire. This kitchen, everything small and narrow and arranged with great attention to detail, almost decorative. This woman did not tolerate anything ugly around her.

Yes, the mayor might well have thought: how can God have created such a creature! And he suspected that the Lord God had not created her so that he could have a grope with her. There must have been a mistake, that Maria ended up in this village. The mayor had been to the distant capital city of Vienna once – Maria would have fitted in there. When she stood up from the chair and pottered to and fro in the kitchen again, the pious musings came to an end and he stared at her behind, watching how it moved, every time she took a step there was a tiny tremor.

On the same day that Josef returned to the war, the mayor stood before the door. In spite of sleet and strong wind, he had made his way up to them. The children were at school. He took off his hobnailed boots, padded in his socks into the kitchen, put on the coffee that he had brought with him for Maria, proper bean coffee. They ate a piece of his wife's cake.

'I am your benefactor,' he said. 'I promised Josef. I keep my promises. However! In times like these, no one can be trusted, not one person, I tell you, not me, not your Josef, your Josef, I tell you Maria, he's a good man but not to be trusted, if I were a bastard, I could denounce him on the spot and he would probably be brought before a court-martial and shot, but who would do such a thing, that is the question, Maria, who would do that, I don't do things like that, I am your benefactor.'

The mayor had spoken in an even tone, without emphasis on any particular word, not even the word 'shot' was emphasised, there was no full stop in his speech until the very end. Maria kissed his hand.

'I don't want that,' he said. 'After all, everything I bring you comes from the heart. To you and the children. It is voluntary. That was not part of the agreement with Josef. That comes direct from my heart. There is no need for social kisses.'

'I don't know what that means,' she said, standing up, which was supposed to be a hint.

'I'll explain it to you another time,' he said and positioned himself close in front of her.

'I don't want that,' she said.

He pushed her sleeves upwards and laid the back of his hand in her bare armpits, pulled her blouse down-wards and tried to reach her breasts. The armholes however were too tight and he swore and tugged. She aimed a blow at him. He grabbed her. She had to be careful that she didn't fall over. She was scared that this was precisely his intention. So that he then fell on top of her. He brought his knee up between her legs and pushed her skirt up. She was unable to free herself, he was clutching her sleeves tightly. She aimed another blow at him, started to panic, got him on the neck. Then she was free and gasped for air.

He apologised to her. If only she would allow him once, just once, he would never touch her again for all eternity. He would swear to it. In times like these it did not matter at all if she allowed him one time, didn't matter at all. In these times, there was no one peering down from heaven at a village like this in a remote valley in the back of beyond. What things did Josef get up to, did she think, in the Italian mountains. Prostitutes were brought into the mountains by the truckload. Whores from all over the place, even from Africa. Black women, the local men can't resist them. Everything is allowed in war. Everyone knows that. Josef wouldn't bear a grudge against her. Even if he knew about it. But he won't know about it. Never. Once was all he asked! One single time! After the war, everything would be different. It would be as if it had never happened. Even the lowest-ranking soldier would be happy if after the war everything that he had done in the war was consigned to oblivion.

'I just want the same as you gave the fellow from Hanover, Maria. Nothing more. Just once, Maria! One time!'

She tore herself away, ran into the bedroom and jammed the back of a chair against the door handle. Keys were non-existent in the Bagage house. At first he carried on, pounding on the door. Then he slunk off.

When the children came home from school and they had all eaten together, she sent Katharina, Walter and Heinrich outside. She gave them jobs to do in the cowshed, in the barn, with the cows, with the goat. She took Lorenz into the bedroom, pulling the door closed behind her.

'Lorenz,' she said, 'you have to protect me. He wants something from me. Don't ask what he wants. You know the answer.'

She did not even have to say who she was talking about. They sat side by side on the bed, mother and son. Lorenz gave a loud snort. He clenched his jaw. You could see it even in the weak light from the tiny window. After a while, Maria says she thinks it might work like this: if he comes, the children should all stay sitting in the kitchen and wait until he goes away again, even if he stays the whole night. Lorenz should sit down where the mayor usually sits and not get up, even if the mayor says he should.

'And if we are at school?' asked Lorenz.

'What if you don't go to school for a while?' asked Maria.

'I can arrange that,' said Lorenz. 'I'll study at home.'

'I can help you,' said Maria.

That evening, as they were all gathered together again around the table, Heinrich, Katharina, Lorenz and Walter, she said: 'Lorenz has something to say to you.'

Lorenz told his siblings all that his mother had told him, didn't try to play things down but also didn't exaggerate.

Katharina said: 'I'll go down and tell his wife, she likes me.'

Lorenz said: 'If you tell her, she won't like you any more.'

Heinrich just lowered his head. Walter glanced from one to another and took everything in. The dog and the cat acted as if they had understood everything too.

Firstly: when and where does the Bagage clan come to an end? Am I still a part of it? Are my children still a part of it? And what about my husband? Secondly: was there happiness and laughter in the Bagage household?

My grandmother used to be high-spirited and good fun on the dance floor when she was a girl before she got married. She came out of herself, as they say, but that was just a couple of times. They used to talk about it a lot though, they liked bringing it up. In the village and in the family too. She liked to sing and was not bad at it, though her sister was actually better. But whenever the two of them sang songs together, it was a joy. They sang in two-part harmony. And occasionally a friend joined them, and the girls sang in three parts. Everyone became reverent for a moment, it was so beautiful. The husband of Maria's sister was a worldly man, that's how they described him. He had lived in Berlin for a year and had lots of stories from this world-famous city. He played the accordion and he enjoyed it when the sisters sang along, he would say in all seriousness, in Berlin they would have a chance of making it. He had brought a song back from the city, it was called 'Baby Doll, You Are the Apple of My Eye'.

And Josef? When he played with the children and pulled the glove puppets over his hands, Mr Punch on his right hand, the crocodile on his left, that was so funny. The children used to laugh. Maria laughed. She had made the puppets herself, sewing them together skilfully. She also sewed shirts, she had even made money from her sewing in the past. Josef used to disguise his voice, first he was Mr Punch, then the cruel crocodile, and then just Papa, simply Papa.

The only time I recall having a real fit of laughter myself was with my second husband. My stomach was sore and I laughed till I cried when he disguised his voice and did impersonations of people.

And my Uncle Lorenz? Did he laugh? Did he ever truly laugh? I have memories of his heavy glasses, they really were heavy – thick lenses, a dark brown frame, I would guess a basic health service frame or one from Russia – you could have easily used them as a paperweight. He was the one who was always centre stage. He had a military bearing about him and yet at the same time he would poke fun at any kind of uniform, even the postman's. When he visited us, my father used to get up awkwardly from his armchair, because of his prosthetic leg, and greet him: 'Here comes the enemy!' I would bring them the chess board, place the pieces on it, hide behind my back a white pawn in one hand and a black in the other and ask Uncle Lorenz to pick. White starts. Then I used to make some tea and serve it. And I put out something sweet to go with it. Always. They never touched it. Ever. Uncle Lorenz put several cubes of sugar in his cup, but they didn't dissolve properly. He drank the tea down in one gulp. The sugar was left in the bottom of the cup. They played for two, three hours, not talking much, and Uncle Lorenz took his leave. 'The enemy departs!' shouted my father. The two were especially close.

I knew that Uncle Lorenz had deserted in Russia during the Second World War, that he had attached himself to the Red Army and had had a Russian wife and child. I had always imagined that his adventurous life would be clear to see somehow, that he would look bold and daring. But no. He was like any other man at that time. According to my father, he had a certain arrogance and found most people thick as two short planks. On the latter point, the two of them agreed with each other. There isn't even a photo of the Russian wife. Nor of the child they had together. Two of his sons grew up to be burglars and one ended his life with a noose. I can remember the twins well. They came to us in the summer holidays, two funny lads, one strong, the other weak. Both of them fancied me. My father always used to say that in better circumstances, Lorenz would have become someone important. Both Lorenz and my father were interested mainly in books and ideas. They liked women who were intelligent and on the same level. My father liked women who were one head shorter than him.

Lorenz, my son, is the opposite of his uncle. He is a painter. He likes to paint animals. Would never shoot at an animal. Once, he was travelling on the underground with a large bucket of emulsion paint and it fell over, full to the brim. He just shrugged his shoulders. Some of the passengers had splashes on their clothes. 'Wash it out straightaway,' was all he said, nothing else. No one got annoyed. Even though he is vehemently opposed to being like his uncle, his uncle would have acted in exactly the same way: he would not have apologised. 'To apologise is to admit guilt', that was a saying that my uncle used often, and sometimes out of context, instead of 'Good morning' or 'Goodbye'. In his studio, my son kneels before the canvas, it looks as if he is swearing an oath to it. Or he takes a brush, fixes it to a pole and walks barefoot over the canvas lying spread out on the floor. He says: 'It's best to make your mind blank, then something appears.' As a child he was never sick. When I was cooking, he used to play in the kitchen, crouching in the gap between the kitchen cabinet and the washing machine, building towers out of empty medicine packets. My Uncle Lorenz was never ill either, his whole life long.

Uncle Heinrich was the one I knew least. If I were to cobble together all he had ever said to me, it wouldn't fill a page. As a child he wanted to have a horse. When he turned forty, he was able to afford one. He bought a Noriker draught horse with an unusual coat, *Tiger*. He had seen the mare at an auction and fallen in love with her at first sight. A very large, very broad animal with hair over her hooves. Uncle Heinrich took me to see her once. I could really see why he loved this animal. He had paid a lot for her. He thought her white coat with the black spots was superb. I did too. As a small boy and as a teenager, Heinrich had always been level-headed and his only interest had been in farming. Neither his parents nor his siblings rated him all that highly, except for his muscle power. As if he were a tractor. He never came to family gatherings. And there was no gossiping about him. Not because there was something to hide. But because there was nothing. He felt closer to animals than people. That had always been the case. Soon after his parents died, he moved away. He was the eldest, and only eighteen, the family home back in the valley was auctioned, and he sought work in a factory. There he met his wife. She was even more self-effacing than he was. She let him feel that he was superior to her. That was important to him, although he never let it show. But all of this is conjecture. Conjecture that my Aunt Kathe put forward. Heinrich and his wife had one daughter and one son. They all scrimped and saved, bought a smallholding and settled in. They were happy and slept the sleep of the righteous. I know little about them. Nothing, in fact. Although Heinrich was never as happy with his wife and children as he was with his horse. The daughter had a good career as an interpreter, I heard, and lived in Paris. Uncle Heinrich had had the horse scarcely two weeks in his stable when it stepped on his bare foot and from that he fell ill. The foot got infected and turned black. His loving wife bound his foot with herbs and was able to save him. He didn't go to the doctor. After the accident, he couldn't stand the horse. His wife looked after the Noriker and whenever Heinrich caught sight of it in the meadow, he closed his eyes and hoped the horse would notice. His foot never recovered completely and this restricted what work he could do. So his wife did almost everything. Heinrich wanted to train up his son to help his mother, but without much success. The son was tired by mid-morning. Once, his daughter came to visit from Paris and brought her son with her. She was dressed very elegantly, her suitcase was of fine leather. The boy was a good-looking lad with black curls. Heinrich then became besotted with the child, persuaded his daughter to leave him here, he would look after him, and that is what he did. He studied together with him, and was convinced that he would make his mark in life. The lad taught Heinrich French and soon they spoke to each other only in that language. Once, Heinrich said to his darling boy, he could have one wish, whatever he wanted, no matter how much it cost, as he had saved quite a lot of money. Then the lad said he would like the Noriker horse as his own.

'*Si je n'ai pas à le regarder,*' said Heinrich and hugged the boy happily.

My Uncle Heinrich had a reconciliation with the horse and shouts of laughter were often to be heard coming from the stable, and neighing – grandfather, grandson and horse.

The next time the mayor entered Maria's house, without knocking, without ringing the bell, Lorenz was sitting in the kitchen where the mayor normally sat. His shotgun was on his knees, he was holding the barrel in one hand, the other lay across the trigger.

'Well look at that,' said the mayor. 'Where's your mother?'

'Not here,' said Lorenz.

'That's no answer.'

Lorenz just looked at him, and said nothing. The mayor could see that the lad was struggling to hold his gaze. Soon it would be midday, there was no smell of cooking. And the table was bare. No plates, no cups, no butter, no milk in a jug, no bread, no bacon, no cheese.

'Nice gun,' said the mayor. 'Do you know how to use it?'

Lorenz nodded. Lowered his head, watched him from under his brows.

'What do you shoot with it?'

Lorenz shrugged his shoulders.

'Birds?'

No answer.

'Something bigger?'

No answer.

'A lovely gun. It shouldn't be used for shooting at stupid targets. Like beer bottles. That would be such a waste.'

Lorenz gripped the weapon more firmly, a sigh escaped him. He stretched his back. He had a curved back, it made him look furtive.

The mayor saw the anxiety in his eyes. 'That gun there, that was made by the best gunsmith far and wide,' he said. 'Do you know who the best gunsmith is?'

Lorenz gave an almost imperceptible nod.

'I know who the best gunsmith is too,' said the mayor. 'That's a Fink shotgun. And Mr Fink, that's me. And now, you young rascal, tell me where your mother is! Or I'll have the gun off you and take the butt to your arse!'

'She's gone to see something,' said Lorenz, but now he shook with rage.

'You're talking like an idiot,' retorted the mayor, pleased to see him shaking. 'Has she gone for a nap? Should I go and have a look? Gone to see something, has she? Aha, what will you do if I go and see some-thing too? If I go into the bedroom and have a look? Are you going to shoot me? You'd better aim well. If you don't get me right in the heart, there will just be a bloody mess and I won't be dead.'

The gun dropped to the ground. Lorenz heaved a sob and ran out into the snow. He was only wearing house slippers on his feet. He ran down to the water trough. Then he turned about and hid in the cowshed and froze there and called softly for the dog, but it had disappeared, and he waited until Katharina and Heinrich came back from school and the dog was there again too and the mayor had already gone.

In the evening, Lorenz told his mother and his siblings what had happened. He didn't describe things worse than they were and he didn't make things better. He said that he had been cowardly and had run away and that he was sorry and it would never happen again. Maria made no comment, but the next morning she told her children to stay at home with her.

'You don't need to go to school any more,' she said. 'No more at all. No more while we are still at war. I can teach you everything you're learning in school. It's nice and cosy when we sit around the table here. It's not so cosy at school, and the truth is, it is easier to learn in a cosy environment. Lorenz can teach you arithmetic. He is just as good at it as the teacher.' Katharina was not to repeat again that it was against the law, please. In war, everything is allowed. Even skiving off school.

Katharina kept her silence.

When my Aunt Kathe finally told the story of the Bagage clan, she could see death approaching, beckoning her. These were her words.

'He is standing there,' she said, and the words came from her face, her mouth scarcely moving, a face like leather. I sat opposite her in her small kitchen in the South Tyrolean Settlement and it seemed to me as if someone was standing behind her doing the talking and she was allowing them to use her face. 'Death is standing there,' she said, 'a few metres in front of me, one foot in front of the other, his skeleton slightly hunched forward, he's turning round to me and beckoning to me to go forward.'

She was already well over ninety by then. A sharp-nosed woman with slender, still well-formed limbs, on her upper arms the sinews of her muscles showed through. A woman, still working as if she were a man and not giving any thought to the woman in herself. An expression of my mother's: 'Katharina, think just for once of the woman in you.' I tried following this, to think of the woman in me. But I never got anywhere, of course. I was only twelve when I heard this expression.

After the death of my grandmother and my grand-father Katharina will care for the family, Lorenz,

Heinrich and Walter, and in addition, Grete, Irma and Sepp who came along later, and every day she will prepare what they eat and make sure that they are all well fed. Katharina will be only eighteen years old.

When Lorenz and Heinrich are taken away for poaching, she will insist on giving them an alibi.

'I swear by Almighty God in heaven and by Saint Katharina and on my own honour and the honour of my siblings that Lorenz and Heinrich were with me all day, sitting in the front room!'

It won't be of any use. No one will believe her. They will think she doesn't believe in Almighty God in heaven nor in her patron saint, nor in any kind of honour, not even in her own. They will be placed in the lock-up, Lorenz seventeen, Heinrich nineteen. The lock-up is to be the mayor's cellar.

There will be a danger that Lorenz will get taken away from them. The mayor will denounce him in front of the gendarmes as the instigator. 'That one,' he will say, 'he is a born criminal.' Katharina will implore Heinrich to take the blame, all the blame, on his own. Lorenz loves his freedom too much, she will say, it's essential for him, he will not survive in a cell. Heinrich will bow to her wishes and admit to everything and swear that he went hunting on his own.

In later years, Kathe will encourage my mother, Grete, not to let men take advantage of her. It is best if she goes out of her way to avoid them.

That's how Katharina will turn out. That was what my Aunt Kathe was like.

That morning – it was the beginning of December, the 4 or 5 December 1914, Aunt Kathe said it would have been one day or two days before Saint Nicholas Day – the children had stayed home again.

And it was just as well that they were with their mother. Katharina, Lorenz and Walter saw the mayor coming up through the snow. Heinrich was in the cowshed feeding the cows and the goat. He saw the mayor too. He threw the hay fork down, left the dog in the cowshed, closed up and ran into the house. He joined his siblings and his mother in the kitchen.

It was quiet. They breathed onto the frost patterns on the windowpane, saw the mayor standing not far from the house. As if he were thinking something over. His head held up and a bit to one side, his chin jutting out. As if he were listening attentively. As if he were checking out the weather. He had a rucksack on his back. He was a black upright lump in the snow. And then suddenly, he was gone. They had not seen him go. He wouldn't have gone up into the woods. As if magicked away. As if erased from the whiteness. And as though descended from heaven, he was standing in the middle of the kitchen. In woollen socks. He smelled of boiled potatoes. Most likely the socks.

Things went differently from what Maria had anticipated. She thought he would back right off when she had them all around her. That at least he would respect the children.

But he yelled down at the children: 'Don't you realise you're going to get locked up? School is compulsory in our country. I am the emperor's representative here! I've come to check up on you . . .' and that they should disappear immediately, immediately. He stamped up and down in his socks in the kitchen. He waved his arms about. He might perhaps turn a blind eye and not charge them but only if they disappeared immediately. If a family broke the rules of compulsory schooling, measures were put in place, the children were to be taken away. That was the law. That was automatic. Even a mayor could do nothing about it. No one should get the idea that laws were no longer valid in wartime. In wartime, laws were particularly necessary. He was shouting so loudly that you could hear it echoing back from the mountain.

'Damnationandtarnationandthedeviltakeyouall!'

He aimed kicks at the children and pushed them, Katharina fell on her side. He pulled Walter by the hair and bundled him off. He hit Heinrich twice on his head with his knuckles, to the right of his ear, to the left of his ear and a smack on the neck. Only with Lorenz did he hold back.

The children ran out of the house, pulling on their winter things as they ran, Katharina was the only one to grab her schoolbag, Lorenz and Heinrich ran without doing up their laces, Walter following behind.

Maria squeezed herself behind the table, ducked down between the corner bench and the table, held up a cushion in front of herself, would have liked to grab any old thing, the candle holder for example, made out of beech wood, but she didn't dare. She thought, it will just make him angrier and he'll tear it out of my hand and kill me with it.

'Now then,' said the mayor and overturned the first chair. 'Now then my fine lady!'

My Aunt Kathe told me what happened next: 'We were running, Heinrich and I, holding hands with Walter, and then Lorenz stopped, the snow-drifts to his left and to his right towering over him. Come on, I called, come on, Lorenz, or else he'll arrest us and we'll be taken away from Mama. I really believed this. People used to say that quite often. About us. In the village, they used to think, not all, but some of them, they thought that the Bagage, that lot up the mountain, the kids are half wild, probably all of them thought it in truth, but some of them actually said it too. We were almost the last people without electricity and without water in the house, just a water trough, and that was twenty metres away and didn't even belong to us. That was what they used to say, hey, they've got all those children and God knows what their father is mixed up in, would it not be better to remove the children so that they at least have a chance of making something of their lives? I was scared, I have to admit. Not Lorenz. If we wanted, we should feel free to carry on running, he called to us, to Heinrich, Walter and me, but he was not going to run away any more. Not him. He turned around and went back. He spread his arms wide and waved them around and hunched his back. We stood motionless for a while. I was really scared, I have to admit, I don't know if I ever felt so scared again in my life, I really don't think so. Everyone in the family knew that once Lorenz lost his temper, he could really let fly. I was almost more scared of Lorenz than I was of the mayor. We stayed where we were until we spotted Lorenz up by the water trough, Heinrich, Walter and I, all together with no caps on our heads, at what must have been minus ten degrees. Of course no gloves, we had left them lying in the kitchen when we ran off in such a hurry. Then we couldn't see Lorenz any more as the snow was piled up so high. I said, let's go, we'll follow him. But we didn't go fast. Heinrich was pulling back. He said, Lorenz doesn't want us to see. What does Lorenz not want us to see, I asked. Heinrich stood still and I went on with Walter, holding his hand. I should at least leave Walter with him, Heinrich called after us. Walter is too young. Too young for what? We carried on. And then Heinrich caught up with us. And as we came into the kitchen, we saw Lorenz. With the gun.'

Lorenz had sneaked up to the house, through the deep snow he went, and round the back of the house, and climbed up onto the roof. That was easy because the house was built into the slope and at the back the roof was almost level with the ground. He knew how to open the skylight from the outside. He first wiped away the snow and then climbed in. He got the gun and appeared suddenly in the kitchen.

'Clear off,' he said. 'I don't need to be a good shot, I'm using pellets.'

This time the mayor did not dare to shout at him. Not this time. Probably because of the pellets. Maria crawled out of the corner and stood behind her son. She laid her hands on his shoulders.

Lorenz raised the weapon to his cheek. 'It's type 00 buckshot,' he said. My Aunt Kathe told me that it was the worst thing imaginable to be shot with pellets. She knew about guns, not as much as Heinrich, and definitely not as much as Lorenz, but she could tell the difference between buckshot and a smooth bullet and she had seen the difference with a deer, and not just once.

'I'm going to count to three,' said Maria. 'After three, I'm going to tell my son to shoot.'

'That would be a serious crime,' said the mayor.

Just at that moment, Katharina, Heinrich and Walter entered the kitchen. Aunt Kathe told me that she just caught the mayor's last words. She started to weep because she thought everything was over for them.

The mayor said, word for word: 'That's it, it's all over.'

'Come close to me,' Maria instructed the children. 'Stand next to me! Everything will be all right. Nothing is going to happen.'

'And all those fine presents I brought you?' asked the mayor. 'What about them? Shall I take them all back again with me?'

'One . . .' said Maria.

'Just take them back!' sobbed Katharina. 'We don't want them. Please take them back! We don't want anything from anybody. Just to be left in peace. We never did anything to anyone.'

The rucksack lay on the table, the straps had been unfastened, a stick of wurst sausage was poking out and two milk loaves and a linen bag of coarse semolina. As if Santa Claus had been to visit.

'And what do you think you're going to live on?' asked the mayor. 'Eating snow won't fill you up.'

'Two . . .' said Maria.

Walter cried out quickly, 'But I want the sausage! At least the sausage. I'm hungry.'

'Take it,' said Lorenz.

'I'm too scared,' said Walter.

'You get it out!' said Maria to Heinrich.

Heinrich pulled the sausage out of the rucksack, looked at the mayor and shrugged his shoulders. The mayor made a gesture, be my guest.

'And the rest, whatever else is in there,' ordered Maria. 'Take it all out!'

At each item, Heinrich looked at the mayor, at each item the mayor nodded.

'Feel free to take it all,' he said. 'It's for you anyway. The bread, the sausage, the *Riebel* corn bake, underneath there is still some cheese and bacon, all for you. You've got your own milk. No thanks necessary. Everything comes from the heart. There is no need to steal things that are gifts.'

Then he got up to go. Very slowly. Took a long time putting on his shoes. Sat down in the middle of the floor to do it. Began to sing a song: 'Mary walked through a wood of thorn . . .'

'Get going!' said Maria.

'Are you going to say three now, because I'm having a bit of difficulty getting my shoes on?' he looked up at her questioningly. 'And you, young man, are you going to shoot the emperor's representative dead, because he's having trouble getting his shoes on?'

He did not look at Lorenz. The mayor had regained a little bit of his dignity. But far from what it had been. He would need many days for that. For the rest of his life, he held Lorenz in respect. He would happily have seen him behind bars.

When the mayor was finally out the door and they couldn't see him outside any more, Maria started to sway and had to hold onto a chair and Katharina ran to her to give her support.

'Get me a glass of water, then I'll be fine,' she said.

But Katharina saw that she was not fine and Heinrich gave her a hand to get their mother into the bedroom. She lay down there and slept until evening.

Maria often had dizzy spells. It didn't necessarily mean anything serious. Occasionally she had fainted. Once in church. That time she had hurt her head. The women had stepped aside. Made space for her and she had banged her forehead on the pew bench.

Walter was also often unwell. He loved his mama so much that he became unwell too. He never put his socks on, always ran around with frozen feet and a runny nose. Lorenz didn't know how to get him to tuck in his shirt front and back, and not to run around barefoot in the cold, not even in the house.

'We can't allow ourselves to be ill!' he said.

He had already had words with Katharina because it was actually her job to look after the little ones. She had just said he shouldn't get so het up. He wasn't their father.

Maria was pregnant. My mother was in her belly.

That December Maria went down every Sunday into the village and to church. That winter almost two metres of snow was piled up on the left- and right-hand sides of the lane and for many days the temperature dipped right down to minus ten degrees, and in between, Foehn storms warmed the air for two days up to as much as twenty degrees. Then overnight the cold rushed back in and snow fell, so that from the driver's seat of the cart, you could not see the horses' ears. Icicles hung from the barn roof like the swords of mountain giants. Day and night the horse drew the snowplough across the paths and the old men, who were of no use in the war, shovelled away; the jingling of the harness could be heard day and night. And one day when everyone was already in church, everyone in their best clothes, women and girls on the left, men and boys on the right, the breath from their mouths turning to steam, steam rising too from the censer in Walter's hands – he had recently become an altar boy, had begged his mother in tears to be allowed to be an altar boy – as he knelt in front of Mary, as the priest had shown the boys, the coil of hair at the back of Maria's head came undone. She took off her shawl and tried to pin her hair up again. What was normally an easy matter proved impossible this time. She could have wept. All the women turned around to look at her. A moan of anguish had escaped her involuntarily. Heartbreaking it was. Lorenz, Heinrich and Katharina had lowered their gaze.

The Bagage were kneeling in the last row at the back. On the women's side. All squeezed in together. Even when Josef was still there, they kneeled, stood and sat at the back of the women's side, two or three empty pews between them and the back row of the rest. Most of the men stood outside during the mass and talked politics, smoked, chewed tobacco and spat, leaving the snow covered with brown stains. At the consecration they came in, kneeled beside their sons, waved a cursory sign of the cross over their faces with an embarrassed look, as if they had been caught in the act of doing something shameful. Josef did not take part in the discussions outside, he stayed with his family, always stayed with his family inside the church. He did not believe in heaven, and not at all in the Catholic Church. He considered all the clergy to be superfluous beings, a waste of space. He did not believe in the saints either, his wife believed in them. Maria believed more in the saints than in the dear Lord, who was too distant and had not experienced life, at least there were stories about the saints. Saint Katharina for example was chained for twelve days, she received nothing to eat from her torturers, and yet she survived, because an angel came in the night and dressed her wounds and brought her bread and milk. During the mass, Josef used to stand there, his long arms hanging down, his hands crossed in front of him, and let his thoughts wander. He remained standing for the consecration too. *Lord, I am not worthy that you enter under my roof, but only say the word and my soul shall be healed.* When the sermon was being given, he would sit down but it was not possible to say whether he was listening or not. He never wore a tie, ever. White shirt. Other men wore checked shirts, on Sundays and on weekdays, on Sunday with a tie though.

Why did my clan always deliberately set themselves apart? Why? Why did they stay so far away, up at the top of the valley? If they didn't want to have anything to do with the others, why did they stay there at all? Maria's brother-in-law and Maria's sister had more than once turned the conversation to a proposal that they could all move to Bregenz, build a large house, set up a business together – the brother-in-law would be the salesman, Josef responsible for the money, for the tax office and the schemes required for keeping the books. Lorenz, with his gift for numbers, would have a future, a future within the family, at his father's side, later taking over from his father. The brother-in-law had not gone to war. He was indispensable at home. He had an important role as a civilian. He had a certificate to this effect. And they were not people to be looked down on, the sister and the brother-in-law, quite the contrary. This even Josef had to admit. The brother-in-law talked a lot, but sense – in comparison to Josef everyone talked a lot. The brother-in-law was successful and respectable. This Josef admitted. Although in general he was of the view that the two things were mutually exclusive.

When Maria was pregnant with my mother, the saints came back into her mind. During this time, she prayed a lot, my Aunt Kathe remembered. Mainly to the Mother of God, who was of course her patron saint. It is easier to talk with a mother. She only learned about Saint Lorenz later on – he was a bit sinister, the one who was roasted to death on an iron grill and had joked about his executioners. If she had known his story earlier, she would have named her son something else. She had never heard of a Saint Heinrich or a Saint Walter. My Aunt Kathe said her mother had reproached herself about this a little bit. But only from time to time. Most of the time anything to do with religion was of no interest to her at all.

'Kathe,' I said – I think I stopped calling her Aunt from when she was about seventy years old, just called her by the short form of her name. 'Kathe.'

'What?'

'Can I ask you something?'

'What?'

'But don't get angry with me.'

'Spit it out! Ask me!'

'Can you be one hundred per cent sure that my mama was your father's?'

'You should get a slapping for asking such a thing!' That was her reply.

'Fine,' I said. 'You said what you were supposed to say. But I'm asking you the same again: was my mother one hundred per cent your sister?'

'One hundred per cent!' said Aunt Kathe. 'You are one hundred per cent one of the Bagage.' Yeah, yeah, she knew just fine what was going on in my strange head, she continued. That her mama had turned to praying because of a guilty conscience. 'That's what you're thinking, isn't it?'

'Pretty much.'

'That's nonsense!'

'And there was nothing between her and the red-headed German from Hanover?'

'No.'

'How can you know all that for sure?'

'I just know, that's all.'

Maria had proclaimed to her sister, back when they were still schoolgirls, that she would one day experience one great love, an overwhelming one that swept her off her feet. Without such a love, the life of a woman was not worth living. Maria's sister had seen the matter through more pragmatic eyes. As a young girl she had already said that a man should offer a woman a good life. A woman could not expect more from a husband. By a good life, she meant a better one than before. That's very modest, Maria had answered to that. At seventeen, Josef had made her an offer of marriage. She was content with this husband. He had given her a better life. Not economically. He was actually less well off than Maria's family. Economically speaking, Josef was a step down. But he gave people respect. Even if he never discussed it – he wouldn't have been able to, he didn't have many words at his disposal – all his instincts were that a person should not be judged by what was jangling in his pocket. From this perspective, he had improved Maria's life. Well, that was a strange perspective, commented her sister. One couldn't sink one's teeth into that perspective. No, true, admitted Maria. Besides, she loved Josef and was already longing for him, but if he didn't return from the war, she would go to Georg in Hanover. On foot if she had to. Why could she not be a different person! There was not a single spider's web in any corner of her house, not a single ball of dust, nothing greasy, nothing sticky, no smelly socks, no sweaty shirts. She would leave behind the tidiest household that one could imagine.

At Christmas in 1914, Josef came home once more, for the last time in the war. Unexpectedly. There were soldiers in the village who had had no leave at all. Whose wives were despairing. One had not received a single bit of news from her husband, not one. She didn't even know if he was still alive. There were soldiers who had not had any leave for four years. They had gone to war for emperor and monarchy, and when they got home, the emperor was dead and the monarchy done away with. Josef was now on his second leave in six months. The general opinion was that Josef had used some of his wheeling and dealing to get it. But no one could have said what kind of wheeling and dealing this might have been, that would allow the poorest farmer from the poorest village of the whole kingdom to bend the great military machine of the emperor in his favour.

The Postadjunkt had trudged through the snow, had called Maria and waved a letter around. An official communication to the wife of a soldier. To be exact, it was not a letter. He would never read a letter, the Adjunkt emphasised, that would go against all sense of decency and duty, this communication had come open without an envelope. Josef had been drawn for a home leave. That's what it said. Typed. With an official stamp.

'Do they draw lots for it?' asked Maria.

'I didn't know they did that either,' said the Adjunkt, out of breath he was and happy. 'You learn something new every day. That's what they say. But we always like to learn good news, don't we?'

Maria was doubtful. 'So it's just chance then?'

'Yes, that's right.'

'Should a leave permit be as much a matter of chance as death?'

'Am I supposed to have a bad conscience because I'm not in the field?' asked the Adjunkt.

'Of course not,' said Maria. And then she overcame all feelings of shame and said: 'Could I ask you a favour?' and turned away so that she didn't have to see the blood rushing into the Adjunkt's face. 'Would you like to come in for a moment?'

She had no idea what to offer him. She really didn't have anything. Nothing at all. Now that the mayor had stopped bringing his gifts, supplies were getting short. Once a week she sent Heinrich or Katharina into the village to buy bread. She still had a little bit of money. Sometimes the woman in the shop, Else, popped a second milk loaf into the rucksack. The side of bacon left as a final gift by the mayor hung down from the ceiling over the kitchen table. The children would rub their chunks of bread over it. So that at least there was a bit of flavour. The Adjunkt loosened his tie and opened his collar. It was warm in the kitchen. There was plenty of wood for the fire. Better to be hungry than cold. That was the motto of the Bagage clan and that is still my motto today.

'Do you promise that you won't say anything to anybody?'

'I promise,' answered the Adjunkt.

'I feel I can confide in you,' she said and took his hand and held it tight, 'because I think you're the most decent man around here.'

'Thank you,' said the Adjunkt. 'But I am sure there are others.'

'No, not one.'

'Well, thank you again.'

'I'm sure you're thinking that I'm only saying that because I want something from you.'

'No, I don't think that,' said the Adjunkt.

Although in reality it was true. 'I am begging,' said Maria.

'I don't understand,' said the Adjunkt.

'I am begging from you.'

He still did not understand.

'I have nothing left.'

Still he didn't get it.

'Nothing left to eat.'

He still didn't understand.

'The children and I, we don't have anything to eat,' she said and had to keep her impatience in check. 'The cows have their hay and the goat too. We have nothing. The dog gets what he needs from somewhere, I don't know where, and the cat too. We only have milk to drink. And if Josef comes home at Christmas, we will have nothing—'

'It will be an honour for me,' interrupted the Adjunkt quickly. That was very thoughtful of him. He wanted to spare her having to go into more exact details about their situation.

This time Josef came for only two days. To be more exact, going by the number of hours, it was just one and a half days. He was exhausted, different, remote, shrunken, weary, uncommunicative, thin, hardly spoke, didn't sleep with his wife, didn't realise she was pregnant. And she didn't mention it. She was two months gone. He didn't want to see anyone outside the family, he said. Any light hurt his eyes.

He needed something to be placed in front of the candles. Contrary to his usual routine, he did not wash himself thoroughly. Everything seemed pointless. The journey over here had been a long one, he said, but good. On the train. He did not say much more. The children kept their distance. When he disappeared again, it was as if he had never been there. You could hardly even see the footprints in the snow from his heavy military boots. Maria found it difficult to recall what her husband had been like before the war. That seemed to her to be a bad sign.

But on the evening of 24 December, they had a roast. Roast pork. With potatoes and sauerkraut. And a bottle of wine. And dried pears. All from the Adjunkt. Maria had thanked him with her tears. They flowed from her as from an actress on the stage. 'Tears on demand.' She had read about it somewhere. The expression too, it had stayed with her. That actresses, amongst other things, had to be able to weep. On demand. When they were teenagers, she and her sister had practised. Her sister never managed it. Maria did though. Her sister would get a fit of the giggles. Maria remembered this when the Adjunkt appeared with the sled. He had pulled it up behind him with a rope over his back. He had tied bags full of good things onto the sled. On top a tarpaulin so no one could see what was on it. She had taken his hand in hers and held it for a long time and looked him right in the eye and commanded the tears to flow and they had flowed. Tears then flowed from the eyes of the good man himself. He could not have had a more beautiful thank-you. Maria's tears were the best Christmas present.

Josef brought money again this time. He gave it to Maria and said that she should keep it safe. She sewed a little linen pouch for each of the family and she shared out the money, Father received the most, the children according to their age, for herself she wanted none. She laid the little pouches under the Christmas tree. Heinrich had cut it down in the forest. The top bent over at the ceiling. On the branches hung cut-out cardboard figures that Maria and the children had made during the evenings with colouring pens. Katharina had borrowed the colouring pens from a school friend. She herself only had one blue one. Six candles burned, one for each member of the family.

'Beautiful,' said Josef. 'Really beautiful. We've got one too. One almost as nice.'

She didn't enquire further.

Once Josef had departed again, Maria kept the pouches with the money under a floorboard. She placed the Christmas tree on top of it.

There was something else, something important! She had baked a sugar cake for Christmas Eve, for the Adjunkt had brought flour and sugar as well. And a lump of yeast with a Christmas greeting from his mother. And a handful of raisins. And butter.

They had wanted to go together to Christmas mass, Josef, Maria, Heinrich, Katharina, Lorenz, Walter, but turned back. Too much snow had fallen, and on Christmas Eve no snowplough would be out, at least not this far up the valley. The singing under the Christmas tree was a bit of an effort, because Walter was the only one who knew the words to 'Silent Night, Holy Night' by heart. Katharina didn't, Heinrich didn't and Lorenz had absolutely no idea. Josef stood there, his arms hanging down, his hands interlaced in front of him. Like in church. It was impossible to see what he was thinking. Walter played with the plaster baby Jesus. It fell to the floor and shattered. That seemed a bad sign to Maria as well.

The couple embraced as they said their goodbyes. But Maria could not bring herself to tell her husband that she was pregnant. She told him in a letter she sent to the field. He wrote back, he didn't think he would get another leave. He was happy about the baby. His mates had broken out the schnapps and toasted him. If it was a boy, he wanted him to be called Josef, like his father.

Father did not return to the house again until the war was over. Sometimes the Adjunkt brought a letter from him. Maria would then send a letter back with him. Josef's letters were seldom longer than four lines. That he was well. That she shouldn't worry. How were the children. That he was looking forward to the end of the war when they could be together as a family again. That things were looking good for the emperor. That was in every letter. It was said that the soldiers were obliged to write that. If they didn't, they would get a severe reprimand. Her replies were just as short.

Soon her belly was showing. Soon everyone in the village had seen Maria Moosbrugger's belly at least once. Where did that come from? Calculations were made. The husband's leave days down to the exact hour. Bearing in mind the condition of a man who comes from the front. Factoring in the favourable and unfavourable times for conception. And this as well and that as well. The outcome did not speak in Maria's favour.

The priest came twice. The first time alone, the second time not alone.

The first time, he said: 'Why do I never see you at confession, Maria?'

She shrugged her shoulders. She had not invited him to sit down at the kitchen table. The priest was of the view that a place was reserved for a man of God in any front room at any time.

'Do you want to have confession now?' he asked.

'Here in the kitchen?' she asked back.

'The grace of the Lord is with us everywhere.'

'No, I don't want confession.'

'Is there nothing you would like to confess, Maria?'

'Do you know something I could confess?' she asked.

Stop! I have to break off here. There has been so much speculation in our family about this conversation between my grandmother and the priest. Each one had his story, no one knew exactly how it had gone. My Uncle Lorenz, for example, maintained that his mother had given the priest a tongue-lashing. I think that was his version because in her place he would have given the priest a tongue-lashing. He was of the same opinion as his father, that someone like that was completely useless, a good-for-nothing. Uncle Heinrich said that their mother had wept, only wept. He remembered that Mama – he still called Maria 'Mama' as an adult, the only one to do so, the others spoke of her as their mother – that Mama during this time had wept from morning till night. So she had wept when the priest was there as well. He, Heinrich, suspected that the priest took her weeping to be an admission of her guilt. Aunt Kathe recalled that the priest, whom she remembered as a particularly unpleasant type, had gone around yelling and calling down the wrath of hell onto the head of their mother and had wanted to force her to admit that the child in her belly was from another man, not from Father, and then Mother had dismissed the priest from the house. Hence the man's evil revenge.

And Aunt Kathe related something else: that in fact Walter, the youngest who was just newly six years old, had run after the priest and confronted him down at the water trough, yes, confronted him, pulled at his black gown and shouted at him, so loudly it could be heard up in the house.

'You're a bad person!' shouted Walter to the priest. 'You'll go to hell!'

The next day the priest was there again, this time not alone, this time with a young lad that he ordered to fetch the ladder from the barn, to climb up and take down the crucifix beside the front door with a crowbar. Inside the house, Maria was cowering in the dark with her children on the matrimonial bed, all of them huddled together. Even Lorenz crawled close to his mother, even he was scared. Although they were not great believers in heaven, and whatever is up on high, they now felt a premonition of danger from that direction, not just from earthly sources.

'You shouldn't have run after him and said he'd go to hell,' whispered Heinrich.

Walter whispered back: 'But I know he is going to hell.'

Maria whispered: 'None of us knows the least little thing about hell.'

'I do,' insisted Walter.

The story spread ever more widely and there was no one who did not know about Maria and the child in her belly, and who did not know the calculations made, all of which clearly pointed the finger at Maria. A lot of unpleasant gossip was circulating. There was a lot going on in the Bagage household. The father's opaque business deals, that no one knew much about. The excessive beauty of his wife. The preference shown to the father as a soldier, because first of all he was still alive, and secondly he'd had leave from the front twice. Then there was Lorenz's more than remarkable ability with mathematics, leaving even the teacher behind. Apparently Lorenz was able to multiply two three-digit numbers in his head in no time at all. No one believed in witchcraft any more, but you never knew.

The mayor was asked about the Bagage household. But he said nothing. Of course, before the war he had been very close to Josef. Those previously mentioned deals. And it was well known that he used to save bits and pieces from his table for her. And one might be forgiven for doubting that he did this for love of his neighbour. Perhaps Josef had something on him. Those business deals. He ought to just come out with it and say what was going on there.

'I am not going to say anything about that,' he said.
'Why not?'
'Just because, you moron!'
'Because you know more?'
'Because I am not going to say anything about it, you moron! You're such a devious lot! A nest of poisonous vipers! The whole village is a complete pile of shit! The lot of you put together are not worth the contents of Josef's spittoon!'

Unfortunately, Aunt Kathe did not tell me the story about Walter running after the priest and confronting him until her brother was long dead. I say unfortunately because I would have liked to congratulate my uncle on this. I think of him with fondness. He was the funniest in the Bagage clan. People claimed that women loved him and desired him and forgave him everything, and that he got any woman he wanted. In my eyes, he was not a handsome man. Maybe the ideal man has changed with the years. He was tall, broad-shouldered and had an athletic figure – although he didn't participate in any sport – with his thin, freckled skin, his red hair – on his arms, on his chest – and on the back of his hands, a pale fluff. He worked less than his brothers, often went on drinking sprees. He chose a compliant wife with a lovely face, who soon grew fat. So he didn't find her attractive any more. They had five children and lived in a house with bare brick walls. He fell for a woman who was on the game. He found this a perfect solution. He never had to justify himself. His lawfully wedded wife took a lover whom she visited often and without embarrassment – he was a sales representative and felt quite at ease with the fat woman. It was she who taught me the foxtrot. When Uncle Walter had grown tired of the prostitute, he passed her on to his youngest brother Sepp, who married her.

The brothers never spoke with each other about the past. They were men who had sprouted up from the ground, who withered when there was nothing more to be expected.

In school, Katharina learned twice as much, twice as fast, twice as confidently, and the teacher respected her. He used to say to the other children, Katharina couldn't really help it if her mother was a whore.

'That's what he said, word for word,' said Aunt Kathe, spitting it out with a hiss, and her angry words sounded more like those of a child than of someone nearly one hundred years old: 'The miserable rat! Saying in front of the whole class our mama was a whore! I hope he's burning down there!'

She had stood there, in front of the class, as the teacher had spoken this way about her mother. Katharina did not trust herself to look up from the floor. The other children didn't want to brush against her. In the cloakroom, they left at least one hook's distance between her jacket and their coats. She had one friend, who secretly gave her bread twists and wrote her little letters in which she said that she was on her side, but was not allowed to show it.

For Heinrich it was his last year at school. He had always been very quiet in class, and the hostility, which he too began to sense, hurt him deeply.

Maria carried Walter in her arms, although he was already far too heavy and would soon be starting school officially, and jumped around with him in the kitchen, making all the cabinets shake. She hoped for a miscarriage, but it was too late for that. She thought she was going to have a girl because she had felt no nausea. She had only ever been nauseous with the boys. With Katharina she had felt a bit dizzy but never nauseous. As if the rumours would have died following a miscarriage.

In July she sent Lorenz to her sister with the urgent request to come and fetch her – it was a matter of life and death. Lorenz set off at four o'clock in the morning. He was at his aunt's house by midday. His uncle harnessed up, and by the evening Maria was at her sister's. She was in good hands. Wrapped in blankets, served with hot tea. With a piece of chocolate on the plate. Lorenz, Katharina, Heinrich and Walter stayed on their own at home. Maria gave birth to a girl. She was baptised in L., it was an informal baptism by Maria's sister because the priest refused. The child was christened with the name Margarethe. Maria was back home within the week.

In the third year of the war, everyone was finding life hard. The Adjunkt and his mother could not spare much any more. Actually, nothing at all. In the summer, apples. One time it was cherries but Maria had cherries herself. He was so ashamed about this that he didn't dare to go up to Maria's any more. She sought him out. He made himself unavailable. From then on, she stopped going to the village. Once, there was a knock on the door. Outside stood a man and a woman. He had his hat pulled down low, and she wore her headscarf pulled tight. At first she did not recognise them, as she pushed aside the curtain in the kitchen. She feared that she would be sworn at again, blamed, cursed, and she didn't open the door, sat on the kitchen floor to avoid being seen, in case the man gave the woman a leg up; she pulled Grete to her and signalled to her to be quiet, which would not have been necessary. Later it turned out that they were a well-meaning couple who had only wanted to say to Maria that they found her to be a respectable woman and would not allow themselves to be riled up by the priest.

One time the priest enquired, from his pulpit, where the Bagage were – usually they were always to be seen in the back pew. But not everyone in the village approved of what the priest had set in motion with his morals. One man, afterwards no one could say who it had been, shouted in the middle of the sermon: 'That's enough now! Stop it!' And another one added, not shouted but muttered, the priest should keep his mouth shut. After all, Josef and Maria were from here, the priest was not a local man.

They were going hungry. And now there were six of them, not including Father.

Little Grete was an easy child. She hardly ever cried and didn't race around. Her favourite place was at her mother's side. Maria lifted her onto her hips, where she clung tight, or took her on her lap and opened up her cardigan and laid it around the child's back and head.

'That can be your little house,' she said.

For Katharina she was a doll. Grete allowed her siblings to do anything with her. She smiled gently and gazed into their eyes. Walter folded a Napoleon hat out of newspaper and put it on her head and stroked her hair out of the way. Heinrich carved a walking stick from a long piece of wooden roof tiling, with a captain's head at the front of it – he was clever at things like that. He pressed it into Grete's little hand. Katharina asked her mama if she could borrow the red material, the nice one, she wouldn't cut into it, it would be a royal cape for Grete. She placed a cushion on either side of the child, left and right on the kitchen table and a third one behind her back. That was the throne. She draped the material over it. Maria had held on to it, at some point she was going to make a dress with it. One doesn't get round to sewing fine dresses for oneself if one's diet includes nothing much more than potatoes and porridge. And anyway, the cloth was a present from the mayor and she didn't like to think about that.

'You are our queen,' said Katharina. At that time, Grete was not even three years old.

'Say: I am a queen!'

Grete said: 'Queen.'

'Say: Queen Grete.'

'Queen Grete.'

'She said it again!' exclaimed Katharina to her mother and cheered.

Queen Grete was my mama. She would definitely not have wanted to be a queen, she did not want to call attention to herself, she wanted to be invisible. When I think of her, I see her lying in bed reading a book. She lies on the sofa in the living room, her eiderdown is a cloud over her body. She was ill, she was nearly always ill. She is in hospital repeatedly, because a part of her has had to be cut out; she gets ever thinner. We didn't visit her in hospital, it was too far away for us. She didn't cook anything apart from chocolate pudding with a dob of butter. We lived in a convalescent home for war-wounded – our father was disabled, one of his legs froze off in Russia. He sat on a truck. He was the manager of the home, he got a salary and we lived there for free. There was a lady who did the cooking for the war-wounded and for us. Just like in well-to-do households.

Our mother lay under her cloud and read a book. The author was Sigrid Undset and the photograph on the dust jacket showed a woman with a plait encircling her head. She looks pretty, a bit chubby, but women were like that then, said our mother. The first sentence in the slim book was: 'I have been unfaithful to my husband.' I remembered that. My mother reads aloud and we understand hardly anything of the story. My sister is nine and I am seven years old. My mother shows no interest in her surroundings, nothing disturbs her, it's as if she's not even there.

I read in a report: *On 23 October 1956 the first armed rebellion in eastern Europe against Soviet rule and communism broke out in Hungary. The intervention of Soviet tanks changed the uprising rapidly into a freedom struggle for national independence.*

Hungarian refugees were given shelter by the convalescent home for war-wounded. Everything had multiple occupants, each chair, each bed. Whole families lay squeezed together in the beds. Every free space had to be utilised. There were now three women working as cooks in the kitchen. Water was steaming for the noodles, fat was spitting. Kitchen maids cleaned vegetables and salad leaves. Every morning, a huge truck stood in front of the house and supplies were unloaded and carried into the cellar. My father was there with a notepad and ticked off every item that was delivered.

Our family, having lived previously in a generous space of five rooms, was now apportioned just two rooms. We had no kitchen, food came up in the catering lift and we fetched it from there and took it to our table. I don't see how it can taste good, said our mother, cooking for so many people requires a professional and our staff were untrained. I say 'our staff', as if they had something to do with us.

Men, women and children sat in the corridors, balls were pushed to and fro. We would peer out of our door with curiosity, but did not dare go out. Strange. Everything was strange. The Hungarian men wore tracksuit bottoms, the way they sat there, they looked as if they were waiting for their match to begin. There was a smell of unwashed clothing and cigarette smoke. Our mother suffered from it. She lit candles and blew them out again. She put twigs of pine wood to one side to dry and when not a drop of moisture remained, she set a match to them. She loved the smell of fresh and of burned pine needles.

In my memory box I found a photograph – I am standing in the middle, with another schoolgirl to my left and to my right, all three of us wearing bathing suits. I was the same age as the other girls but the smallest. That was during the period when our mother stayed in hospital all the time, and I thought about her while the photo was being taken. We did not know what was wrong with her, didn't know that she would soon die, and then when she actually died, we found it hard to believe. Strangers stroked our heads and said: 'Oh you poor children, four of you without a mother.' That was really awful. We had visited her in hospital and she'd looked full of life, almost euphoric one might say. Now I know, that came from the morphine. Soon she felt sick, and we were sent out of the room.

In my class two schillings fifty was collected from each child to buy a wreath; it was embarrassing for me, and I would have happily jumped out the window to be spared the experience. Then I could have died and gone to heaven with her.

When Grete died, her brothers and sisters were still alive. Queen Grete was the first. And when it happened, the bottom fell out of our world, her sisters and brothers, her children, my two sisters and my brother, it was as if we hadn't known that she was very ill, as if there was no illness that led to death, as if death itself did not exist. I will never forget that day. A friend told me about the dog she had received as a present. She was desperate to show him to me. Now. Right now. I was to go with her to her house, admire the dog, and then run on home for lunch at my aunt's. My sisters and I were living at that time with my Aunt Kathe, because our mother was in hospital. It was going to be boiled potatoes with carrots and a piece of stewed steak with all the goodness leached out of it after being used to flavour the soup – the strands of meat always got stuck in your teeth. It was a Saturday. When I arrived home, I saw my sister banging her head against the wall, Aunt Kathe was weeping into the soup, I had no idea what had happened. Then they told me the news in a whisper. Our mother had died. 'Grete is dead.'

And then it was winter again. And they had absolutely nothing left. Not even a side of bacon hanging
from the kitchen ceiling. The last of the potatoes
were inedible.

Outside it was snowing. It was snowing so hard
that you couldn't see the water trough from the
kitchen. Lorenz came back from school. It was afternoon. He shook the snow out of his hair and laid
his school things down in the kitchen. Nodded a
greeting to his mother who had Grete on her lap
as always. Katharina and Walter were doing their
homework. Lorenz went into the cowshed, said to
Heinrich he should leave it to him, he should go
back into the house and take some firewood with
him. Heinrich did not contradict his brother these
days. He called the dog and disappeared with him.
And didn't question. Lorenz waited. Stamped his
feet warm. He wanted to wait long enough for it to
start getting dark across the mountain. Then he went
ahead with what he had planned in the night down
to the smallest detail. He had made preparations
in advance, had deposited two thick pairs of socks in
the barn that morning, also his father's thick gloves,
a second shirt and a pair of long johns, normally
he never wore those. Somehow they seemed to be
a sign of cowardice, he didn't know how else to
put it. Now in the barn he pulled everything on
and put on the cap with the fur-lined ear mufflers,
which also belonged to his father. Sat down on the

shaft of the wheelbarrow and inserted his feet into his father's mountain boots. They were too big for him, but no longer far too big; with a second pair of socks on his feet, they were fine. Lastly, he worked his arms through the straps of the large rucksack that smelled mouldy and was not used because there was nowhere for them to get enough supplies to warrant using it, the small rucksack was always sufficient. Then he stamped off out of the house and took the narrow, trodden-down path in the snow past the water trough, down to the paved road. He continued along it into the village, his head held down against the snow still falling from the heavens, and marched through the village right to the last farm on the other side. He whistled loudly as he went, even sang a few verses aloud. No one was around outside at that time, had someone been outside, Lorenz would have greeted him, almost overly enthusiastically, that's what he had decided to do. If it were to happen, then they should recall that he was quite open, not acting in a suspicious manner at all. That Lorenz from the Bagage, he's in a cheery mood today, that's what anyone meeting him should think. A cheerful person is no threat. No one came across his path. In this driving snow, no one left their living room. But perhaps someone was looking out of the window. Definitely someone would be looking out of their window. They would see him, no threat to anyone, cheery in spite of the weather.

In the last house, at the other end of the village, lived one of his classmates, the only one who Lorenz had contact with from time to time. Actually he quite liked him, but my Uncle Lorenz was already of the firm belief that he was someone who kept himself aloof from everyone and on that basis could not really find another person likeable. Not even Emil. Although he did somehow like him. He helped him with arithmetic homework and more than once got him a better mark. As he got to the house, it was dark. He knocked with the iron ring on the door.

Emil's mother opened up. Quickly Lorenz pulled the cap from his head, so that she would see who it was and not have to ask first or feel scared.

'What do you want?' she asked, without greeting him by name.

This he felt was rude. A flash of rage mounted up to his neck but he managed to restrain it at his Adam's apple. He swallowed and tried to be as cheerful as he could. He couldn't find his reading book at home. Grete must have gone and lost it, the baby lost everything. He would most likely find it tomorrow, but probably not until the end of school, and in school tomorrow he had to read two pages aloud, and unfortunately he was not very good at reading. One person can be good at arithmetic, another at reading. He would prefer to be good at reading . . . and so on. He talked as he had planned the night before and practised silently. Even if it was a load of drivel, what he was saying, that was exactly what he had planned. It was all calculated. He knew Emil's mother, he knew that she admired him because of his gift for arithmetic but that she also envied him because this was exactly the subject that her Emil was weak in. So he had worked out that she would be pleased, if he made out that he, for his part, envied Emil his reading skills.

'I wanted to ask Emil if he would lend me the reading book until tomorrow.'

The things people said about Lorenz's family were not all that complimentary, in fact the exact opposite. Some people believed them; some people didn't believe them. Some people believed them but still drew a line at the behaviour of the priest acting as if he were above even the Lord himself. The Bagage children went to school just when they felt like it, just when it suited them. Yes, one had to criticise them for that. Maria never bothered too much about anything. You didn't see her around the village any more either. She was too standoffish. Emil's father rebuked his wife over and over again. She should stop with that imagination, what did she know about anything, and just because the mother of the Bagage clan was better looking than the lot of them – yes, the whole lot – that was no reason for nastiness. But where there's smoke there's fire, his wife retorted. But even so, she would not have removed the crucifix.

'Wait a minute,' the wife said to Lorenz.

Once again, she did not address him by name and did not invite him into the house, a further discourtesy in his eyes. An insult. The door was closed in his face. It was snowing so hard that in the few minutes since he had taken off his cap, a white fleece had settled on his hair. It was no way to treat anyone, not even a beggar. He froze, kicked his shoes against each other. Emil stretched his head round the door and gave him the book and an apple as well. The dog, a light-coloured animal, pressed his nose between Emil's knee and the door post. He allowed Lorenz to stroke him, a tame dog that was not much use for anything. Lorenz tucked the book into his belt above his belly and, pulling his knitted jumper over it, trudged off.

He took the path homewards. If they are watching me, they'll see me going the normal way. Down the middle of the paved road. His footprints could no longer be seen, the snow had already covered them. Once he was out of sight, before he came to the houses that were set closer together in the main part of the village, he climbed over the fence beside the path. He could hardly be seen because he disappeared into the pile of snow that the snowplough had dredged up. He jumped from the fence into the snow on the other side and sank into it up to his chest. He struggled across the field and up to the woods, in summer it would not have taken more than five minutes, now a good quarter of an hour. On all fours he crawled the last, steep section into the forest. The forest was so dense here, there was just a dusting of snow between the trunks. He needed to get his breath back, knelt down, brushed off the snow, shook out his cap and his gloves. Then he went through the woods back to the house in which Emil and his family lived. The cowshed and the barn were built on at the back. In the front room you couldn't see or hear what was going on in the cowshed or in the barn.

From the edge of the woods to the cowshed was no more than ten metres. But through a ditch in which the snow was collecting. At the first step, Lorenz slipped down and sank completely. As he tried to right himself, he was still submerged under the snow. For a moment, he felt fear, even panic, that he was going to suffocate. He swept his arms around in a swimming motion. The snow penetrated between his cap and his collar, his face glowed from the cold, but he carried on sweeping with his arms, thrashed around, held his breath, and finally poked his head out of the snow. I'll never be able to come back here again, he thought. He struggled on until he reached the barn. Under the overhang of the roof, he dusted the snow from his clothes and cap and gloves. He was exhausted, his legs felt numb above his feet, as if he didn't have any at all. And his lungs were sore. He felt like swearing but he didn't dare, he knew himself too well, once he started with the swearing, he lost control.

Then above him he heard:'Zi–zi–zizizi! Zi–zi–zizizi!'

A chaffinch sat on the lower cowshed roof. It hadn't seen him. He knew all the birds by their call. 'Fly away home, or you'll freeze,' he said softly.

A squirrel hopped in front of his feet, out of the barn.

'Go home or you'll freeze,' he said to this creature too.

The slope down from the woods shimmered through the fallen snow. There were no tracks to be seen. He hadn't foreseen that he would have to swim his way through a blanket of snow, now he thought it was a stroke of luck. No one would discover any tracks. No one would suspect him. This was the plan that my Uncle Lorenz had hatched the night before, as he lay next to his brother Heinrich in bed: if I go to Emil, quite openly, and sweet-talk his mother, it won't occur to anyone that Lorenz Moosbrugger was the thief. Because no one will believe that someone could be so brazen. Not even one of the Bagage could be so brazen. If, however, I don't go there first, if they simply notice that something has been stolen, then the first thing they will think is that it was one of the Bagage, and most likely, Lorenz. Even if it hadn't been me, that's what they would think. The stuff about the book was a diversionary tactic. People are never more easily distracted than when they are being flattered. Uncle Lorenz was proud of this observation. He would laugh about it right to the day of his death, Aunt Kathe told me.

He broke into the barn and along into the cowshed and sneaked from the cowshed into the cellar of the house. In it, sides of bacon were hanging from the ceiling, wheels of cheese were piled up on shelves. These people had stocked up, well of course, they had the wherewithal to stock up. There were glass jars with preserves, pears, apples, pickled cabbage, pickled pumpkin, potted meat, damson compote, cherry compote. He piled as much as he could into the rucksack. Until it was so heavy he could hardly lift it. Then he crawled through the tunnel under the snow, and across the ditch up to the forest, and in the forest he went parallel to the main street below, dragging the rucksack, had to keep stopping to catch his breath. Up higher, where the paved road ended and the climb up to their house began, he trampled out a hole in the snow and laid his booty inside. Then he trudged through the snow with the empty rucksack and retraced his steps through the woods until he was back above Emil's house.

Lorenz climbed into the house of Emil's parents five times that night. He cleared out the whole larder, he left them not a single glass jar of preserves. He took cheese, sausage, bread. And the snow fell from the sky all the while and obliterated his tracks. On his last trip he stuffed three hens into the rucksack. He had already built a hutch for them some days before in the cowshed behind the cows. When he had finally finished, it was two in the morning. His fingers were so numb that had he injured them, he would have felt nothing. He did not have the energy to make it into bed. He lay down on the kitchen floor. Fully clothed. The woolly earmuffs on his head, the two pairs of gloves on his hands, his father's mountain boots on his feet.

But he didn't skip school the next day. In the morning he told his mother nothing about where he had been and what he had been doing. And Maria did not question him further. She could rely on her Lorenz. Whatever he did, he did for the benefit of his family. He asked her if she could iron the reading book, it had got crinkled and it didn't belong to him and he had to return it today. She filled glowing embers into the smoothing iron, laid a cloth over the book and afterwards it looked almost like new again.

After school, Lorenz commandeered his siblings into helping him bring the provisions up from the hole in the snow. Lorenz had even thought in advance about how to hide things in the house. Just in case someone had the idea that it had been one of the Bagage household that had broken into Emil's parents' house. Maybe no one had the idea, or if they did, they were so intimidated by the Bagage that they kept their traps shut and looked the other way.

My Aunt Kathe told me that her brother had once said to her, he had never experienced such a wonderful feeling in his whole life as the way his mother had looked at him that day. That day had been the best day of his life. And his mother had never looked more beautiful than on that day. And he had never been happier than on that day. The whole afternoon, he lay on the bench by the stove and slept. One of the hens had broken its wing, Maria wrung its neck and plucked it and made a soup with it. She wrapped a warmed blanket around her sleeping son's feet and covered him up. That evening there was a feast. There was nothing anyone could teach Lorenz after that. He knew how to survive. And no one could tell him any different, no one.

The war ended in November 1918. But Josef did not come home until Christmas. The mayor was no longer mayor. There was no mayor any more. No one in the village knew exactly what the political situation was. Everyone had grown thin. The soldiers who returned had all gone grey or even white, even those who were not yet thirty years old.

Josef got hold of the mayor.

'What's with all this talk?' he asked.

Josef had not gone grey. He had a black beard down to the middle of his chest and looked terrifying. Eyes as hollow as empty egg cups with a button burning inside each one, no one had ever seen anything like it. He had greeted the children and ignored his wife. And ignored Margarethe. He had sat in the trough where the snow still lay on the edges and scrubbed himself down with a large brush that he had brought with him. He had also brought some fresh things, civilian things: a soft, checked shirt, fine flannel, new; a pair of corduroy trousers, also new, with a brown leather belt pulled tight; an Italian jacket with a herringbone pattern, also new. Everything new. He had put on a tie – it matched the checked shirt as though the two items had been chosen at the same time and with professional advice. Even the rucksack was new, not just any old rucksack out of canvas but a leather one, soft leather. No one asked who had given him the things, where he had bought them, and if so, where did he get the money, and he wasn't giving anything away. Rejuvenated, he went down into the village and got hold of the mayor. 'What's it all about?'

'All what?'

'You know exactly what I'm talking about. Why the priest took down the crucifix, that's what.'

'What is going on about what! You keep beating around the bush and you don't even have the courage to say outright what you mean.'

'That the brat is not mine. That's what I mean.'

'Who says that?'

'What's the story?'

'You want to know something from me?' said the former mayor, now known only as Gottlieb Fink. 'I want to know something from you. So what should we do? Do we answer each other? Who is saying that?'

'I met someone back in Innsbruck, he told me. I didn't know him. He said it was common knowledge. Even he knew about it. And he isn't even anything to do with us. And even he knew.'

'And who is supposed to be the father of little Grete? Can't you even say her name? She doesn't do you any harm. Who is it supposed to be?'

'I'm asking you. That's exactly what I am asking you, Mr Mayor.'

'I'm not mayor any more. I'm Gottlieb Fink, nothing more.'

'Then I am asking Gottlieb Fink – is the brat mine?'

'I know you've just come back from the war and I know war doesn't do much to improve a man's character, rather the opposite, but I would prefer it if you didn't call her a brat in my presence. Call her by her name. She's just a child, and nothing more, but she's still a person and has a name. Her name is Margarethe, Grete for short.'

This is how I imagine – how I would like to imagine – that Gottlieb Fink spoke to Josef Moosbrugger. Aunt Kathe outlived all her siblings, and I had kept putting off my investigations until she was the only one still alive. I myself would never have used this word. Aunt Kathe had called them that – 'investigations'.

'Do you want to come and visit me because you are doing your investigations?' she had asked me on the phone.

And so I had said: 'Yes, I want to do some investigations. One has the right to be curious about one's origins.' And could I come and see her.

Once she had decided to tell the story, she did it in a lively way. And I mean lively. Literally. She acted as if the people she was talking about were still alive, and not only that, as if they were at this moment having a conversation in her kitchen in the South Tyrolean Settlement.

I asked: 'What did my grandfather say when he came home from the war and saw little Grete, my mother?'

And Aunt Kathe: 'What did he say? What do you think he said? Nothing, he said nothing. He went down to the village and got hold of Fink.'

'And what did he say to Fink?'

And she: 'What do you think he said to Fink? What is all this talk about? That's what he'll have said.'

'And what did Fink say?'

'What do you think Fink said? He'll have said: what talk? I can't imagine he would have said anything else. And Papa, what will he have said? He'll have said that the brat is not mine. And Fink will have said: don't call the child a brat. The child's name is Margarethe, Grete. You have to learn how to behave again when you come home from war, Josef. That's how Fink would have spoken. I can't imagine it any differently.'

My Aunt Kathe played out this conversation between Josef and Gottlieb Fink in front of me. Not as if she had been there. But as if it were taking place right here and now. That was her style. That's what I mean by lively.

During their conversation, a big lie was told, a really big lie. Aunt Kathe was so sure that such a lie could not have been planned, she attributes it to a spur-of-the-moment impulse from the devil.

She did not know what got into Gottlieb Fink, said Aunt Kathe. For a while, things had been going to and fro between him and Josef, getting hostile. Josef felt hostile, firstly because at that time, so close to the end of the war, he was hostile to everyone, like most of the soldiers probably were. But he was especially hostile to Gottlieb Fink, because, if the rumours were true, Fink had not watched out for his wife. Josef took the man to task, with the harshest words – she couldn't imagine it went otherwise, said Aunt Kathe. And Gottlieb Fink answered him.

'What goes on in your head, Josef?' said Gottlieb Fink, who was mayor right up to the end of the war. 'What has been going on in your head? Did you think, I'll give Gottlieb an order and he'll just carry it out? I never heard a please from you, Josef, or a thank-you. The lord and master doesn't stoop so low.'

'You don't need to lecture me,' said Josef. 'I want to know something, just one thing actually – is it true that there was a German with Maria in the house? Was there a German?'

'And now the lord and master comes back from war,' Gottlieb Fink continued as if he had not been interrupted, 'and immediately starts acting like a policeman with the right to conduct hearings. And goes on about a German. And is implying that I, notwithstanding my role as mayor at that time, that I had neglected to take care of things. That I should have prevented a German from visiting Maria.'

'Did he visit her?'

'No,' said the mayor. That was the first lie. He knew of course that the man from Hanover had been up in the house. He had seen him himself. And he repeated: 'No, he wasn't up in the house.'

'Does that mean there was no German?'

'No, there was a German. But not at Maria's.'

'But he is the brat's father,' said Josef.

'I'm telling you again,' the mayor burst out, perhaps he grabbed him by the collar of the new sports jacket with the herringbone pattern, 'the child is not a brat, and her name is Margarethe, Grete. And no, the German is not her father.'

'Who is then?'

And at this point, said Aunt Kathe, something took hold of the mayor. She could not imagine it other-wise. This was the big lie. And she could not imagine that Gottlieb Fink had planned in advance to tell such a big lie. The devil had prompted him on the spur of the moment.

Gottlieb Fink, the former mayor, said: 'The child is mine. Grete is my child. Margarethe is my daughter.'

And he had carried on speaking, had held Josef back at arm's length and grabbed him at the same time, maybe this time really gripping the collar of the fine sports jacket with the herringbone pattern. And my Aunt Kathe, who was uncertain her whole life whether God existed, was certain of this – that the devil put the following words into the mouth of Gottlieb Fink:

'What goes on in your head then, Josef? Instead of falling to your knees on the earth of your homeland and thanking the Lord God that you have survived this miserable war without losing a leg or an arm or an eye, you come rolling back from Innsbruck where some rogue has put a flea in your ear and you start haranguing me. Do I ask you where you got this smart jacket from? Or the smart trousers and the good leather belt? Yes, I have an eye for these things. You give me your lovely wife to look after, fine. What do you think I am? Am I a block of wood? That would be news to me. I am human and more than that, a man. And your wife Maria, and I warn you, don't take it out on her, not even a light slap. Is she a block of wood? She is a woman. Well, you self-satisfied soldier who's just lost a war, do you think a woman like that is here only for you? No one else is allowed even to look at her? That's what he thinks, the self-satisfied soldier who's just lost a war. A man is a good man if he can look after a woman. And I'm able to do that. You can't. Even if you say now it isn't your fault, the fact remains. I shook my fist in the face of all the rumours, yes, let me be frank. I defended your wife, I defended her against abuse and against hunger too, please don't forget that. But I was not able to defend her from the manly instincts in myself. And that's enough now, Josef! Go home and act like a man who knows how to look after his family!'

That's how it must have been, said Aunt Kathe, she could not imagine it being any other way.

For a while, perhaps until Easter, but perhaps not quite so long, Maria and Grete slept in the double bed, and Josef on the bench by the stove in the kitchen. For a while, Josef did not speak to Maria. He no longer had any dealings with Gottlieb Fink. Instead he travelled more frequently on the new bus to L. to see his brother-in-law. He quite often stayed overnight. Soon he was sleeping in the double bed again. And he didn't say anything if Grete was there too. But she was not to lie in the middle, in the dip. He would not say her name. Not once. And he never, never looked at her. And never, ever directed a single word to her. He acted as if she was not in the house. None of the siblings dared to confront their father about it, not even Lorenz. Katharina looked after the child, but mainly she clung to her mother's skirt tails. Maria was soon pregnant again. She gave birth to a daughter and named her Irma. Maria went into the village more often again. In the shop she chatted with Else and other women and no one would have noticed any difference between her and the others. The child had black eyes and everyone said she resembled her mother a lot. Maria kept quiet at this, for she thought she knew what people were saying and what they were thinking. She had sworn to Josef on her life and the lives of her children that Grete was his child and that she could not be anyone else's – unless, like with Mother Mary, God had attempted a second pregnancy without a man. He didn't believe her. She told him everything. That a man from Hanover had approached her in the market in L. because he wanted some information. She had spoken to him and people had been watching and that's where the rumour had started that had thrown such a big shadow over the whole village during the war. She told him that Gottlieb had made advances to her, that she had almost been unable to tear herself away from him, but that in the end she had torn herself away. She said nothing about Lorenz – about him defending her with the gun, or about him stealing for the family. She could see how Lorenz was afraid of his father.

He wasn't afraid of anyone or anything in the world, she thought, except for his father.

Once again, Maria became pregnant, and this time she felt nauseous, she vomited every day and grew thin, and her hair fell out when she brushed it. It was a boy. He was christened Josef. That's what his father had wanted. His whole life long everyone knew him as Sepp.

Maria, my grandmother, was thirty-two years old and had given birth to seven children.

And then she fell ill. Her belly became swollen, you could hear her screams. Josef got someone to phone the doctor. He discovered that her appendix was on the wrong side. Maria died. A month after the first stab of pain.

Twelve months later, Josef died. From blood poisoning. He had injured himself cutting wood. At the end, when he lay in his black suit on the bench by the stove, shivering with fever and no longer able to stand, the mayor had come. Spirits had descended on him in the night, he said, and had threatened to torment him day and night without end until his distant death, if he did not tell the truth. The truth was nothing had ever happened between him and Maria. He had desired her, but Maria had pushed him away. She had not given him the slightest spark of encouragement, no, not the slightest, nor the man from Hanover, Maria had been the most loyal wife to walk the earth since the Mother of God. Grete was his child, Josef's, no one else's.

Her father, said Aunt Kathe, had listened and nodded. She did not know if he understood. By the next day he was dead. And they, the children, were alone: Heinrich nineteen, Katharina eighteen, Lorenz seventeen, Walter thirteen, Grete seven, Irma three, Sepp two.

The children sat on the double bed, one beside the other. The dog lay at their feet. The cat was snuggling up on Grete's lap. Birds were gathering outside the window. It was spring. The Foehn wind blew its scents in through the cracks. A blue tit pecked a hole in the ring of fat and sunflower seeds. Katharina had put out small pieces of apple for the blackbirds. Robins and chaffinches froze in terror as a sparrow-hawk flew overhead. A jay pecked at a dried *Riebel* corn bake on the veranda. Then it went quiet.

'When the blackbird sings . . .' said Grete, but didn't continue, as if something else had suddenly occurred to her.

Walter and Grete were the ones with the fine fair hair. In amongst the dark siblings the two of them looked as if they were from a different family.

Their parents were still a living presence in the walls, their mother in the bed frame and the mattress. Her smell was in the clothes she had left lying there. One might have thought that they had been set out there for her. She is about to come out of the bedroom and get dressed. Heinrich tried on his father's new clothes, the ones that were not black, because Katharina told him to, but he did not feel comfortable in them. They would have been best suited to Walter but they were still too big for him. Irma asked if she could borrow her mother's scarf, the one with the fringes; it smells of her.

Lorenz had observed the hunters. Had crept along behind them. He wanted to know when they went hunting. And how long they went out for. He wanted to go hunting with Heinrich and Walter when the coast was clear. It was simply a matter of feeding themselves. Those were Aunt Kathe's words: 'In those days it was simply a matter of feeding ourselves.'

Lorenz had taken possession of the Fink shotgun. It was his. No one had ever contested that. Lorenz would shoot. Heinrich and Walter were to be the beaters, driving the prey into his line of sight. He would shoot a roe deer or a chamois. Heinrich and Walter had to wrap the prize in the big blanket and carry it back home. Lorenz would go along beside them, the shotgun not slung over his shoulder but at the ready in his hands. Rabbit was always on the table. Heinrich was not quite sure which birds could be eaten. Could you eat blackbirds? They would have been the easiest to kill. They settled in front of you in the grass and looked straight into the barrel of the gun. You couldn't eat birds of prey, that was clear. Sparrows didn't have enough meat on them. There were no doves around here. Lorenz dreamed of a stag. A couple of times he'd had one within shooting distance. He would have wanted to keep the antlers for himself and haul them around with him all his life, wherever life might take him, and if he had known that it would take him to Russia in a second war, where he would desert and start a second family, he would have said: the antlers are coming with me! But my Uncle Lorenz never did shoot a stag.

Hunters had come within shooting distance too. They had called out and waved their arms.

'Hey you, young Bagage!' they called out. 'Young Bagage, we're shooting here.'

It was the first time he had been addressed by this name. It meant: they respected him. And: they expected him to behave accordingly. To show himself worthy of their respect. If he had slipped off, they would have lost their respect for him. He raised the gun, laid his cheek against the butt and aimed at them.

'Bagage,' they called. 'We're shooting today!'

That could only mean: tomorrow it's your turn. What else could it mean? And that meant: we are equals, we're not better than you, you're not better than us, we are on the same level, only you are standing on one side and we are on the other.

'Put the gun away!' they called.

His heart pounded and he hoped the hunters could not see how his jacket was shaking over his heart. He held his position, did not put the gun away. So they turned round. And departed. That could only mean: today you shoot, tomorrow we shoot. The opposite way round. So he had won. He went home, slowly, as if he were twenty years older or one hundred years older, a mountain spirit that unexpectedly appears in the forest, that the hunters respect and for whom they leave the field free for that day. When he got to the water trough, he called out to Heinrich and Walter. And from that day onwards the word among the hunters was: when the young Bagage are in the forest, go home! Watch out!

There was no one in the village who would not have been in awe of Lorenz, no one in the village who was not in awe of the Bagage. They became the Bagage proper only after the death of their parents. No one was in any doubt that Lorenz would shoot any man who tried to prevent him looking after his siblings. But also, no one was in any doubt that sooner or later, they would end up in prison. All of them, the whole lot. Because they were scum. In spite of everything, they were scum. Pious women saw them as having something of the devil about them. If God had loved these children, He wouldn't have taken their mother and father from them so soon.

Irma with her black eyes spun around in front of the mirror and thought she looked very beautiful. She was thin and looked more like her father. Her pale face was also like his. She had big plans for herself. She wanted to marry a rich man and so enable the family to have a better life. That's not how it would work out. She was to fall in love at the age of seventeen with a teacher who was married. She would dream of him coming into her bed, such a big dreamer. When Katharina and Grete had been married for some time, she was still single and waiting for the teacher's wife to die. Various men had been after her. She gave them all short shrift except for a theology student that she dissuaded from joining the priesthood. She accepted him and everyone was surprised that he should be the one to succeed in taming the temperamental Irma. She became timid and in the end always looked to him for approval. He was loud, overly loud. When he spoke, each and every word could be heard two houses away, and there were some horrible words, and when he laughed the crockery rattled in the cupboards. He was a carer in a home for orphans, an expert in the godly. He was not one for rules; soon he had a second wife and lived alternately with Irma and with the other one. A lonely old neighbour left him her house in her will. Because he was such a good person. A very loud person, very uncouth, but a good person. Who spoke with God. Hence the loud voice. He took the property and Irma was ashamed when she bumped into the angry heirs in the street. The loud man became blind and learned to be a masseur and was very popular with the women he massaged in the cellar.

At some point, when they were still the Bagage and lived back up the valley, before the house was auctioned, Irma had the idea that the family – now it included just the siblings, Heinrich, Katharina, Lorenz, Walter, Grete, herself and little Sepp – could emigrate to America. That was when they had absolutely nothing left. She had read that they were looking for people in North Dakota. You were given some land and some timber to build a house. Her siblings didn't want to go, and going alone would have been too lonely. When the loud man appeared on the scene, the pipe dreams were forgotten.

The girls, when they were still the Bagage, often sat on the bench in front of the last house before the mountain, and sang in three-part harmony, so beautifully that the Postadjunkt was moved to tears. Now Maria was no more, he felt inconsolable, he hadn't got over the death of this beautiful woman. He often went to her grave when it was dark and brought flowers or sprigs of foliage. He sat at the edge of the woods, listening to her children singing, imagined himself as part of the family, and marvelled at the graveside at how beautifully Katharina, Margarethe and Irma could sing. On feast days he would put small gifts by their door. They were not supposed to know who had left them. But they knew. Once Irma gave him a big hug when one of the gifts was a bracelet. It was wrapped in paper, her name was on it. Irma was for him the most beautiful now that Maria was no more. But she was not as beautiful as her mother. No woman on earth could ever be as beautiful as Maria Moosbrugger.

And my Uncle Sepp? When he was born, his father was happy and paced up and down with him in the house. Little Josef would follow in his footsteps, he would complete what his father had started. But unfortunately that was not to be. What was it that his father had started? Josef, who was first known as a baby by the name Seppele, then later by the name Sepp, was a weak man. With the fine features of a girl. He was not much interested in women. If Walter, the ladies' man, had one to spare, he passed her on to his brother Josef. So my Uncle Sepp was left with the prostitute from the Rhine Bridge. She brought him no happiness. She bore him a girl, Michaela with the golden curls. She tried to jump from a window when she was thirteen. Sepp got a divorce and handed over the girl to his sister Katharina. She wanted to make sure that Michaela trod the right path and didn't turn out like her mother. Michaela though became addicted to heroin, fell ill with AIDS and died. There's a film for schools about AIDS. She plays the lead role. It is shown as a warning.

When my Uncle Sepp lay dying, I visited him. He was almost see-through.

In the Art History Museum in Vienna, I had a look at the painting *Children's Games* by Pieter Bruegel the Elder and there they all were, all the Bagage clan. They were dashing about all over the picture, laughing and whining, shrieking at one another, or whispering, and I stood in front of it and burst out laughing.

'Try to do a pirouette!' says Irma to Grete. Grete would rather leave her legs dangling in the water.

Walter builds a sandcastle for Seppele, but he feels he is too old for this game; he would rather balance a hat on a stick.

'I challenge you to a wrestling match,' Lorenz goads his brother, who is just returning from the animals.

'We could play marbles afterwards,' suggests Heinrich.

'Not till you've washed,' says Lorenz.

In school, the boys want to do *bench pushing*. That's when someone has to get pushed off the bench. It's always the cry-baby, the weakling, the one they all laugh at.

The schoolgirls are playing 'Swan, Stick On!', a version of catch. Grete stands at the pear tree, the girls pull at her hair and call out: 'Swan, stick on!' But she starts crying and won't play any more.

'Let's see who can pee the farthest,' says Walter to Lorenz, and Walter wins.

Who is going to give Seppele a piggyback? Who's got the ball?

'Come on, let's get some twigs for the fire!' calls Katharina.

'If we're not going to church any more, we could play processions at home,' says Irma. 'Grete can scatter the flowers, Katharina can take the crucifix from the wall and march out in front, the boys can carry Seppele and pretend he is Baby Jesus.'

'I'd rather shoot at the picture on the wall, I could shoot at the eye on the face in the picture,' says Lorenz scornfully.

'You're not allowed to, it's a picture of the Holy Mother,' says Seppele, who is wearing a blue cape and wants to be a woman.

'Come on, let's get to bed,' says Katharina. 'It's already past midnight.'

Nearly all of the people I am writing about are in their graves. I am old too. My children are still alive, except for Paula who only lived to twenty-one. I often go to her grave and say, see, I visit you far more often now than if you were alive. I would have felt embarrassed to visit you so often. You would have opened the door and said: 'Oh, Mama, it's you again.'

A Note on the Author and Translator

MONIKA HELFER grew up in Vorarlberg, Austria. Her novels include the Schubart Prize-winning *Die Bagage* (*Last House Before the Mountain*) and the Johann Beer Prize-winning *Die Bar im Freien*. She has been awarded the Bodensee and Solothurn Literature Prizes, the Johann Peter Hebel Prize, and the Austrian Cross of Honour. This is her first novel translated into English. She lives in Hohenems, Austria.

GILLIAN DAVIDSON is a translator based in London. She studied French and German at Edinburgh University. This is her first published work of translation.

A Note on the Type

The text of this book is set in Bembo, which was first used in 1495 by the Venetian printer Aldus Manutius for Cardinal Bembo's *De Aetna*. The original types were cut for Manutius by Francesco Griffo. Bembo was one of the types used by Claude Garamond (1480–1561) as a model for his Romain de l'Université, and so it was a forerunner of what became the standard European type for the following two centuries. Its modern form follows the original types and was designed for Monotype in 1929.